Brander Matthews, Charles Lamb

Dramatic essays

Brander Matthews, Charles Lamb

Dramatic essays

ISBN/EAN: 9783337303686

Printed in Europe, USA, Canada, Australia, Japan

Cover: Foto ©Andreas Hilbeck / pixelio.de

More available books at **www.hansebooks.com**

THE

DRAMATIC ESSAYS

OF

CHARLES LAMB

EDITED WITH AN INTRODUCTION AND NOTES BY

BRANDER MATTHEWS

London

CHATTO & WINDUS, PICCADILLY

1891

This Selection,

FROM THE WRITINGS OF AN AUTHOR WHOM
WE BOTH LOVE, IS INSCRIBED TO

LAURENCE HUTTON,

BY HIS FRIEND AND FELLOW-WORKER,

THE EDITOR.

CONTENTS.

vi   *Contents.*

INTRODUCTION.

CHARLES LAMB AND THE THEATRE.

AMERICANS take a peculiar delight in the humour of Charles Lamb, for he is one of the foremost of American humourists. On the roll which is headed by Benjamin Franklin, and on which the latest signatures were made by Mark Twain and Mr. Bret Harte, no name shines more brightly than Lamb's. By the captious it may be objected that he was not an American at all ; but surely this should not be remembered to his discredit, — it was a mere accident of birth. Elia could have taken out his naturalization papers at any time. It is related that once a worthy Scotchman, commenting on the well-known fact that all the greatest British authors had come from the far side of the Tweed, and citing in proof thereof the names of Burns and Byron and Scott, was met by the query whether Shakspeare was a Scotchman also. Reluctantly enough it was acknowledged that he was not, — although he had parts not unworthy of that honour. So it is

with Charles Lamb.   He was an Englishman ;
nay, more, a Cockney, — indeed, a Cockney
of the strictest sect ; but he had parts not unworthy of American adoption.   He had humour,
high and dry, like that which England is wont
to import from America in the original package.
At times this humour has the same savor of irrev-
erence toward things held sacred by commonplace humanity.   Charles Lamb never hesitated
to speak disrespectfully of the Equator, and he
was forever girding at the ordinary degrees of
latitude.   His jests were as smooth as they
seemed reckless.   He had a gift of impertur-
bable exaggeration ; his inventive mendacity
was beyond all praise ; he took a proper pride
in his ingenious fabrications, — and these are all
characteristics of the humour to be found freely
along the inlets and by the hills of New England
and on the prairies and in the sierras of the
boundless West.   He had a full sense of his
high standing as a matter-of-lie man.   Moreover, he had a distaste for the straight way and
the broad road, and he had a delight in a quiet
tramp along the by-path which pleased him personally, — a quality relished in a new country,
where a man may blaze out a track through the
woods for himself, and where academic and
even scholastic methods have hard work to hold

their own.   Even his mercantile training, in so
far as it might be detected, was in his favour in
a land whose merchants are princes.   And behind the mask were the features of a true man,
shrewd, keen, and quick in his judgments ; one
who might make his way in the New World as
in the Old.   There is something in the man, as
in the writer, which lets him keep step to a
Yankee tune.   Wordsworth wrote, —

> And you must love him ere to you
> He will seem worthy of your love.

The Americans loved Lamb, early, as they did
Carlyle and Praed, — to name two, as dissimilar
as may be, of the many British writers who have
found their first full appreciation across the
Atlantic.   Charles Lamb's only acted play met
in America a far different fate from that which
befell it in England ; and I have a notion that
his writings were aforetime, and are to-day,
more widely read in these United States than
in Great Britain.

"Truly was our excellent friend of the genuine
line of Yorick," said Leigh Hunt ; and although
the phrase is not altogether happy, it serves to
recall two of Lamb's chief characteristics, —
his humour, and his love of the stage in general
and of Shakspeare in particular.   That Lamb

was fond of the theatre admits of no dispute, though he was wont to chide his mistress freely. For Shakspeare he had an affection as deep as it was broad. Whenever these two passions crossed each other, the theatre must needs to the wall, — as in the suggestive and paradoxical essay 'On the Tragedies of Shakspeare, considered with Reference to their Fitness for Stage Representation.' Yet that essay yields in charm to Elia's delightful papers ' On Some of the Old Actors,' ' On the Acting of Munden,' and ' On the Artificial Comedy of the Last Century.' This last essay it was which Macaulay thought worth while to refute solemnly and at length. I have an idea that if Lamb could have read this posthumous refutation, he would have longed to get his hands on Macaulay's bumps to examine his phrenological development.

Lamb's humour has an Oriental extravagance to be expected in one who signed himself ' Of the India House ; ' but his phrase had always a clerkly and clean-shaven precision not a little deceptive. In him, as in any other humourist, unusual allowance must be made for the personal equation. A humourist sees things as no one else does. He notes a tiny truth, and he likes it, and straightway he raises it to the nth, and, lo ! it is a paradox. He never meant seriously that the Restoration Comedies are sound and wholesome works, as refreshing in their austere morality as the Fathers. Nor does he believe that it is a sin to set Shakspeare's plays on the stage, though a simple-minded reader might think so. The light plays of Wycherley and of Farquhar did not offend Charles Lamb, and the wit delighted him. To him the comedies of Shakspeare lost somewhat of their range and elevation when seen across the footlights of the stage. A true lover of Shakspeare from his youth up, he could see more in his mind's eye than the most lavish and learned of stage-managers could give him. But there are relatively few students of Shakspeare, and the mass of common humanity had no mind's eye ; it can see only with the eye of the body, and if its sluggish imagination is to stir at all it must be moved by physical means. In the theatre alone is found the sovran magic which makes the familiar yet shadowy figures of Shakspeare live and move and start from the printed page into actual existence in the flesh.

Lamb's liking for the drama and for all things pertaining to the drama was second only to his love for Shakspeare. The ever-delightful ' Tales from Shakspeare,' over which he toiled despairingly, — little masterpieces which amply repaid his travail, — are scarcely more labors of love than the 'Specimens of English Dramatic Poets who lived about the time of Shakspeare.' To Lamb, more than to any other, is due the revival of interest in the Elizabethan dramatists. It was the fresh discovery of these old dramatic poets that gave him the impulse to write 'John Woodvil.' In the modern drama even the inferior contemporary farces were not despised, and some of them are remembered now only because Lamb saw Munden act in them. Once or twice he took up the pen of the regular dramatic critic to bear witness against the play of the hour. Even then he is as gentle almost as when he recalls the comedians of an earlier day ; he was not one of those fierce critics who, in Douglas Jerrold's phrase, review a play 'as an east wind reviews an apple-tree.' The acted drama, the actual stage of the present, was always of interest to Lamb, and served not seldom to suggest happy illustrations for his notes on the poetic drama of the past.

It is difficult for any one who has had to read much of the writings of other dramatic critics to speak of Charles Lamb's essays on theatrical subjects without falling into the extravagance of eulogy, the very midsummer madness of praise.

There were in his day two other lovers of the
theatre, able men both of them, having knowledge of the stage and insight and imagination, —
Hazlitt and Leigh Hunt. But what are they
beside Charles Lamb ? Coleridge bids us " compare Charles Lamb's exquisite criticisms on
Shakspeare with Hazlitt's round and round imi-
tations of them ; " and to Leigh Hunt such a
comparison would be still less favourable. Indeed, there is but one who has written about
the English stage at all worthy to be set beside
Charles Lamb, and he is the author of an
' Apology for the Life of Colley Cibber.' Like
Boswell, Cibber was personally contemptible
enough ; and like Boswell, he had the unknown
art to make a great book, unequalled of its kind.
There are two grand portrait galleries of the
British theatre, and it is not easy to say which
is the more artful a painter of players, — Colley
Cibber or Charles Lamb. Besides the full-
length portraits of Betterton, Mrs. Barry, and
Mrs. Bracegirdle, — speaking likenesses every
one of them, soundly drawn and mellow in color,
as we see them in the ' Apology,' — may be
placed the group from ' Twelfth Night,' which
we find in the ' Essays of Elia,' — Mrs. Jordan
as Viola, Bensley as Malvolio, Dodd as Sir
Andrew, and Dickey Suett as the Clown. And

Cibber of course was wholly without the boundless humour that has depicted for us a few of
the five hundred faces of Munden, and cap-
tured on canvas a glimpse of Elliston, "joyousest
of once embodied spirits."

Although only one of Lamb's dramatic pieces
got itself acted at last, all of them were written
for the stage. He never gave in to the heresy
of the unactable drama. His plays were intended to be played, as Shakspeare's were, and
Marlowe's and Chapman's, and those of the
other great men whom he loved and lived with.
To him, as to them, a play which could not be
played was no play at all. A 'Drama for the
Closet' is surely a patent absurdity, — *bon à
mettre au cabinet*, in Molière's phrase. Lamb
was too keen-sighted in matters of literature not
to know that form is of the essence of art,
and that therefore every literary effort must con-
form to its purpose. He would never have
accepted the latter-day theory that there are two
kinds of drama, — that intended to be acted, and
that not intended to be acted. He was fond of
paradox, no doubt ; but it would be a paradox
too much for even his stomach that a string of
decasyllabic dialogues, lacking the relief, the
colour, and the movement needed by the stage,
should declare itself to be a drama.

Unfortunately, the serious drama of Lamb's day was empty and inept ; and so he went back for his model to the Elizabethans. He did not consider that the change in the physical conditions of the theatre forced a change in the form of the drama. The turbulent throng which stood of an afternoon in the uncovered pit of the Globe Theatre to see a boy Lady Macbeth act before a curtain declaring itself to be a royal palace, was very different from the decorous audience which sat in Drury Lane to gaze in wonder at the decorations and illuminations contrived by De Lutherbourg for the ' Christmas Tale ' of David Garrick. The stage has its changing evolutions, like society; but Lamb, though he might confess the change, did not feel it. " Hang the age ! " he cried ; " I 'll write for antiquity."

Now, Shakspeare if he were alive would not write for antiquity. As a practical man, he would make skilful use of every modern improvement. Knowing how needful it is to catch the eye of the public, he would turn to advantage all later devices of scenery and stage-mechanism and electric-lighting. Indeed, I doubt not that were Shakspeare writing for the stage nowadays there would not be wanting dramatic critics to say that he was too " sensa-

tional ! " and to intimate that he catered to the
taste of the gallery. Of a truth — if the digres-
sion may be pardoned — ' Hamlet ' is a very
sensational play ; it has a ghost and a duel and
no end of fighting, and an indiscriminate slaughter
at the end ; and before that consummation a
young lady goes mad in white muslin, and there
is a clown at the burying, and a fight over her
grave. It has something more and other than
these physical facts ; it has that within which
passeth show. But it has the show-part — the
mere appeal to the eye — as very few plays
have. And in this quality ' Macbeth ' and
' Romeo and Juliet ' are but little inferior to
' Hamlet.' They could, every one of them, be
acted in dumb show before a company of
miners just out from the mouth of the coal-pit,
and the story would be followed with interest.

This is what Théophile Gautier had in mind
when he said that the skeleton of every good
drama is a pantomime. Action, of course, is
only the bare bones of a play, and must be covered with the living flesh of poetry. There can
be no true life in a piece unless it has a solid
skeleton, — a play may even exist with but a
scant clothing of verbiage, as we may see in any
vulgar melodrama ; but the finest poetry cannot
give life to a drama unless the bones of its story

are well knit and well jointed. This is what the
Elizabethans intuitively understood, in spite of
the rudeness of their stage. This is what Lamb
seems never to have been able to achieve. In
externals, ' John Woodvil ' is at times strangely
like a minor work of a minor fellow-dramatist of
Shakspeare. We do not wonder that Godwin,
happening unawares on the lines —

> To see the sun to bed and to arise,
> Like some hot amorist with glowing eyes —

came to Lamb to ask in which of the old dramatists they might be found. In internal structure,
however, there is nothing Elizabethan in ' John
Woodvil ; ' there is no backbone of action, — the
story is invertebrate.

Lamb knew his own deficiencies in this respect, though he did not recognize their extent
or their importance. He wrote to Mrs. Shelley,
in 1827, while he was engaged on ' The Pawnbroker's Daughter,' that he could do the dialogue
readily enough, " but the damned plot, — I believe I must omit it altogether. The scenes
come one after another like geese, not mar-
shalled like cranes or a Hyde Park review. . . .
I want some Howard Payne to sketch a skeleton
of artfully-succeeding scenes through a whole
play, as the courses are arranged in a cookery-

B

book, I to find wit, passion, sentiment, character,
and the like trifles ; to lay in the dead colours, —
I 'd Titianesque 'em up ; to mark the channel in
a cheek (smooth or furrowed, yours or mine),
and where tears should course, I 'd draw the
water down ; to say where a joke should come
in, or a pun be left out ; to bring my personæ
on and off like a Beau Nash, and I 'd Franken-
stein them there ; to bring three together on the
stage at once, — they are so shy with me that I
can get no more than two, and there they stand
until it is the time, without being the season, to
withdraw them."

This is a free confession that Lamb did not
know the rudiments of the playwright's trade.
Bating a jot here and there for the exaggeration
of the humourist, we may accept this account of
his failings as fairly exact.   But though he could
not help himself, he could give excellent advice
to his neighbour.   William Godwin did not
lose heart after the untimely taking off of
his ' Antonio,' most humourously chronicled by
Lamb.   He got ready another tragedy, which
Kemble declined ; and he sketched out a third,
which was submitted to Lamb for suggestions.
In these Lamb was fertile ; and though the seed
he dropped fell on stony ground, much of it was
worthy of a richer soil.   There is a letter of his

wherein he develops out of his friend's feeble plot a strong situation, almost identical with the second act of the ' Lucrèce Borgia ' of Victor Hugo. And in a preceding letter he had hit upon a situation very like that on which turns the plot of the operatic ' La Favorita.' These two letters of Lamb's should be studied by all who seek for success on the stage. They are full not only of that criticism of life which is the only true criticism of literature, but of a knowledge of stage-devices, and of the means whereby an audience may be taken captive, very remarkable in one who could not apply his precepts in his own practice and for his own benefit.

Here, for instance, are a few of Lamb's dramatic dicta : " Some such way seems dramatic, and speaks to the eye. . . . These ocular scenes are so many great landmarks, rememberable headlands, and lighthouses in the voyage. Macbeth's witch has a good advice to a magic writer what to do with his spectator : —

> Show his eyes, and grieve his heart.

You must not open any of the truth to Dawley by means of a letter : a letter is a feeble messenger on the stage. Somebody, the son of his, must, as a *coup de main*, be exasperated, and obliged to tell the husband.

"I am for introducing situations, sorts of counterparts to situations, which have been tried in other plays, — like, but not the same. On this principle I recommended a friend like Horatio in ' The Fair Penitent ; ' and on this principle I recommend a situation like Othello with relation to Desdemona's intercession to Cassio.   By-scenes may likewise receive hints. The son may see his mother at a mask or feast, — as Romeo, Juliet.   The festivity of the company contrasts with the strong perturbations of the individual.   Dawley may be told his wife's past unchastity at a mask, by some witch-character, — as Macbeth upon the heath, in dark sentences. This may stir his brain and be forgot, but come in aid of stronger proof hereafter.   From this what you will perhaps call whimsical way of counterparting, this honest stealing and original mode of plagiarism, much yet, I think, remains to be sucked.

"I am certain that you must mix up some strong ingredients of distress to give a savour to your pottage.   Your hero must *kill a man*, or *do something*."   Earlier in the same letter Lamb had said, " A tragic auditory wants *blood*," and had warned Godwin not to disappoint them of the tragic ending.

After all, there is nothing so very unusual in

the fact that as a critic he knew what ought to
be done, although as a dramatist he could not
do it. Charles Lamb was a genius, and William
Godwin was not ; but from a seat in the pit
'John Woodvil,' which was never acted, is
little or no better a play than 'Antonio,' which
was damned.

"I am the worst hand in the world at a plot,"
writes Lamb to Godwin ; and we can call 'John
Woodvil' to bear witness to his truth. Strictly
speaking, Lamb's tragedy has no plot, although
it has a story. It lacks the chain of closely
linked incidents and situations which we are
wont to demand in a play. The merits of
'John Woodvil' are poetic merely, and dramatic only by accident or in incidentals.

A word or two here as to Lamb's poetry may
be in place. It may be doubted whether, in
any strict use of the word, Lamb was a poet at
all ; but as I write this the memory comes back
of 'Hester,' and of 'The Old Familiar Faces,'
and of certain passages in 'John Woodvil,' and
it seems a harsh judgment. De Quincey, a
kindly critic, who credited Lamb's prose with the
"rarest felicity of finish and expression," called
his verse "very pretty, very elegant, very tender,
very beautiful," but thought that he was as one to
whom the writing of verse "was a secondary

and occasional function ; not his original and
natural vocation, — not an ἔργον, but a πάρεργον."
In short, Lamb had his poetic impulses and his
poetic moments, but they were not long-lived.
In verse, as in prose, he had always something
to say ; and he said it aptly, with care.   His is
not the polished verse that reflects only the
empty image of its writer.   Nor is he like that
French poet of whom Malibran used to speak,
and who was rich in words and poor in ideas ;
so the great singer described him as " trying to
make a vapor-bath with a single drop of water."
Lamb did not try to make a vapor-bath, and he
was never reduced to a single drop of water.

Of ' John Woodvil,' the minor characters re-
veal themselves in their deeds, and they are
grouped skilfully to set off the hero.   But the
hero himself is not a man of action, — he is an
elegant conversationalist.   How Kemble must
have longed for the fine speeches which John
Woodvil pours forth !   They were full of a true
poetry he could well appreciate, and exactly
suited to his cast of thought and histrionic habit.
Yet he was right to reject the play, even had he
not had ' Antonio ' as a warning.   There is not
much to act in ' Woodvil.'   The man does little
or nothing ; he talks and stalks, and talks again ;
once he seems about to get drunk, which might

enliven the story somewhat, and once he fights a duel ; but as he spares his adversary's life, even this pleasing incident lacks finish. The end of the drama is tame beyond endurance on the stage. If, however, we put down our opera-glasses, and read ' John Woodvil ' quietly by the fireside, there is much to reward us. The character of Margaret is beautifully presented and developed. She is akin to Shakspeare's women both in character and in adventure. Even the manly disguise she does is a frequent Elizabethan, and indeed Shakspearian, device. The dialogue throughout is full of the tricks of the older dramatists, especially a frequent dropping into rhyme.

At the time Lamb wrote ' John Woodvil ' he was in the fresh flush of his delight in the plays of Beaumont and Fletcher, and of Marlowe. In the joy of his discovery of these poets and of their fellows, and in the heat of the imitative fever this gave him consciously or unconsciously, he wrote, besides the tragedy, a dramatic sketch called 'The Witch.' This fills a scant three pages in the collected edition of his poems, but it is an extraordinary production. It might be a fragment recovered from a lost play by the author of 'The Duchess of Malfy' or 'The White Devil.' It has the secret, black, and midnight atmosphere. 'The Witch' is as Elizabethan as

' John Woodvil ' in external language, and even more so in the internal feeling and thought.

Two other of Lamb's dramatic attempts may be dismissed briefly before taking the one play of his which did undergo the ordeal by fire, and was seen by the light of the lamps. One of these was 'The Wife's Trial,' or ' The Intruding Widow,' which the author declared to be a dramatic poem founded on Mr. Crabbe's tale of ' The Confident.' It is a story in dialogue rather than a play, although certain passages in it might not act ill. The other theatrical effort was ' The Pawnbroker's Daughter,' a farce in two acts. This was founded on his own essay ' On the Inconvenience of being Hanged.' It was written nearly a score of years after ' Mr. H.,' and from a letter to Southey it seems as though there was once some hope of its being acted at the Haymarket Theatre. " 'T is an extravaganza,' wrote Lamb, " and like enough to follow ' Mr. H.' " ' The Pawnbroker's Daughter ' is a very whimsical piece. Like 'Mr. H.,' it was quite the equal of the average farce of the first quarter of this century. To us its fault is that it is not above this average. Cutlet is an amusing character, and so is Pendulous : in each of these are to be seen strokes of Lamb's genuine humour. At the fall of the curtain comes the dramatic millennium, when everybody forgives and forgets, and is happy.

The one play of Lamb's known to everybody is the two-act farce called ' Mr. H.,' acted at Drury Lane Theatre, December 10, 1806, and damned out of hand. " These are our failures," said Mr. Brummel's valet ; and ' Mr. H.' is, in England, always accounted one of Lamb's failures, and quite the worst of them. It was acted but one night. The prologue was received with great favour, and Lamb, who was sitting with his sister in the front row of the pit, joined in the applause. The curtain fell silently at the end of the first act. During the second, some of the spectators began to hiss, and Lamb went with the crowd, "and hissed and hooted as loudly as any of his neighbours." Talfourd tells us that Elliston, who played ' Mr. H.,' would have tried it again, but " Lamb saw at once that the case was hopeless."

The farce has not been performed since in England, to my knowledge, save twice only. It was given at an amateur performance in 1822, by the late Charles James Mathews, when the young architect who was one day to be Elliston's legitimate successor as the airiest of light comedians, acted in this play, which had been damned at Drury Lane, and in another, which had been

damned at Covent Garden, — both of these mis-
fortunes being duly set forth on the play-bill
with characteristically impudent humour. And
it was given once again some sixty years later at
the Gaiety Theatre in London, at a single mati-
née, by a little band of enthusiastic young actors
and actresses calling themselves " The Dramatic
Students." And these are the only two appearances of ' Mr. H.' on the English stage.

The consensus of British criticism is that
' Mr. H.' was too slight for the theatre and too
wire-drawn in its humour, and that its failure
was what might have been expected. From
this view an American, for reasons to be given
hereafter, feels called upon to dissent. No
doubt ' Mr. H.' is not one of the author's richest
works ; nor, on the other hand, is it as barren
and bare as its critics have declared. To my
mind, ' Mr. H.' is not at all a bad farce, as the
farces of the time go : in 1806 a popular farce
was not required to be as substantial and as
instructive as a tragedy. It has scarcely action
enough for two acts ; but it is no slighter in plot
and situation than the flimsy five-act comedies of
Frederick Reynolds, whose ' Dramatist ' and
' Notoriety ' were very well received in their
day and are carefully forgotten in ours. It is
" well cut," as the French phrase it, — well

planned, well laid out. In the first act is the
wonder, the perplexity, the guessing, the questioning as to the name hidden behind this single
aspirate. In the second we have the unexpected
disclosure, the general repulse, and the happy
deliverance. The dialogue is actable ; it is fairly
good stage dialogue, lending itself to the art of
the actor ; and while it is not in Lamb's best
manner, it is of far higher literary quality than can
be found in the faded after-pieces of that time,
or in the more highly coloured farces of our day.
The fault of the piece, the fatal fault, was the
keeping of the secret from the spectators. To
keep a secret is a misconception of true theatrical effect, an improper method of sustaining dramatic suspense. An audience is interested not
in what the end may be, but in the means
whereby that end is to be reached. Before the
play was done, Lamb wrote to Manning (then
in China) that " the whole depends on the
manner in which the name is brought out." If
the audience that night had been slyly let into
the secret in an early scene, they would have
had double enjoyment in watching the futile en-
deavours of the *dramatis personæ* to divine it,
and they would not have been disappointed when
Mr. Hogsflesh let slip his full patronymic.
Kept in ignorance, the spectators joined the

actors in speculation ; and when the word was revealed they were not amused by the disgust of the actors, so annoyed were they that they had been puzzled by a vulgar name.

Perhaps, too, there was a certain reaction after the undue expectancy raised by the prologue. Lamb wrote to Wordsworth that the number of friends they " had in the house . . . was astonishing." Now, nothing is so dangerous on the first night of a new play as a large number of the author's friends in the audience. One is greatly inclined to regret that Lamb did not yield to Elliston, and let the play be acted again. If it had had a second chance, the injudicious friends would have been absent, and the name of the hero would have been noised abroad, — and once in the possession of this secret, the audience might well have laughed long and heartily at the hero's misadventures.

The reason that an American hazards this supposition is simply that the experiment was tried in these United States, and with success. Three months after ' Mr. H.' was seen at Drury Lane it was brought out in New York, at the Park Theatre, where it was acted for the first time March 16, 1807. It seems to have made no great hit and no marked failure. Mr. Ireland, whose ' Records of the New York Stage ' is the model book of its kind, — erudite, ample, and exact, — finds no record of the repetition of ' Mr. H.' until 1824, when it was performed " by desire." In 1812, however, it had been produced by the very remarkable company then gathered at the Chestnut Street Theatre of Philadelphia. Mr. William B. Wood, one of the managers of the theatre, acted Mr. H., and in the highly interesting volume of histrionic autobiography which he published in 1854, under the title of ' Personal Recollections of the Stage,' he records the result in one brief and pregnant paragraph : " Charles Lamb's excellent farce of ' Mr. H.' met with extraordinary success, and was played an unusual number of nights." Mr. Ireland has found that Wood continued to act the part for ten or a dozen years. I can hope only doubtfully that some tidings of the better fate that befell ' Mr. H.' here beside the Hudson and the Schuylkill was borne across the Atlantic to the attic near the Thames where Lamb received his friends of a Wednesday evening ; but I fear me greatly this good news did not venture on the wintry voyage, or some record of his pride at this unexpected reversal of the London verdict by the higher court of Philadelphia would linger in one of the many letters to Manning.

" And so I go creeping on," Lamb wrote to
Manning, " since I was lamed by that cursed
fall from off the top of Drury Lane Theatre into
the pit, something more than a year ago. However, I have been free of the house ever since,
and the house was pretty free with me on that
occasion."

It cannot be doubted that this freedom of the
theatre was a precious privilege to one like
Lamb, who had no great store of wealth. In
1817 he moved to Russell Street, with Drury
Lane in sight from the front window, and Covent
Garden from the back ; and here he lived for
six years, almost within sound of the orchestras
of the two patent houses, almost within hearing
of the double tinkle of the bell that rolled up
the great green curtain. It was perhaps the
right of admission purchased by ' Mr. H.' which
gave him the chance to study certain of the old
actors about whom Elia was to discourse in days
to come with ample humour and exact knowledge. To the end Elliston, who had acted Mr.
H., remained a prime favourite. To the end
the play-house was for Lamb a haven of rest ;
for there, as he looked across the smoky flare of
the footlights into the mystic recesses beyond,
he could forget himself, and find surcease of
sorrow, relief from haunting dread, and recrea-

tion after "that dry drudgery at the desk's dead wood."

The hour came when Lamb was released from doing his daily stent of labour; but that hour took away perhaps as much as it brought. Comrades began to drop by the wayside; on the stage also the ranks of the old favourites were thinning; and even behind the curtain Lamb missed "the old familiar faces." The hour came when Mary Lamb, who had worked with him over the ' Tales from Shakspeare,' and who had sat by him in the pit at the hissing of ' Mr. H.,' was more and more shut out from him in the darkness of a clouded mind. The hour came when Coleridge, the friend to whom he had tied himself in youth, was taken from him. The hour came to Charles Lamb at last, as it must come to all of us, when —

> We speak of friends and their fortunes,
> And of what they did and said,
> Till the dead alone seem living,
> And the living alone seem dead.
>
> And at last we hardly distinguish
> Between the ghosts and the guests,
> And a mist and shadow of sadness
> Steals over our merriest jests.

BRANDER MATTHEWS.

THE

DRAMATIC ESSAYS

OF

CHARLES LAMB.

c

THE DRAMATIC ESSAYS

OF

CHARLES LAMB.

MY FIRST PLAY.

AT the north end of Cross Court there yet stands a portal, of some architectural pretensions, though reduced to humble use, serving at present for an entrance to a printing-office. This old doorway, if you are young, reader, you may not know was the identical pit entrance to old Drury, — Garrick's Drury, — all of it that is left. I never pass it without shaking some forty years from off my shoulders, recurring to the evening when I passed through it to see *my first play*. The afternoon had been wet, and the condition of our going (the elder folks and myself) was, that the rain should cease. With what a beating heart did I watch from the window the puddles, from the stillness of which I was taught to prognosticate the desired cessation! I seem to remember the last spurt, and the glee with which I ran to announce it.

We went with orders, which my godfather F. had sent us. He kept the oil-shop

(now Davies's) at the corner of Featherstone
Buildings, in Holborn. F. was a tall, grave
person, lofty in speech, and had pretensions
above his rank. He associated in those days
with John Palmer the comedian, whose gait
and bearing he seemed to copy, — if John (which
is quite as likely) did not rather borrow somewhat of his manner from my godfather. He
was also known to and visited by Sheridan.
It was to his house in Holborn that young
Brinsley brought his first wife on her elope-
ment with him from a boarding-school at Bath,
— the beautiful Maria Linley. My parents
were present (over a quadrille table) when he
arrived in the evening with his harmonious
charge. From either of these connections it
may be inferred that my godfather could command an order for the then Drury Lane Theatre
at pleasure, — and, indeed, a pretty liberal issue
of those cheap billets, in Brinsley's easy auto-
graph, I have heard him say, was the sole remu-
neration which he had received for many years'
nightly illumination of the orchestra and various
avenues of that theatre. And he was content it
should be so ; the honour of Sheridan's familiarity — or supposed familiarity — was better to
my godfather than money.

F. was the most gentlemanly of oilmen, —

grandiloquent, yet courteous. His delivery of
the commonest matters of fact was Ciceronian.
He had two Latin words almost constantly in
his mouth (how odd sounds Latin from an
oilman's lips!), which my better knowledge
since has enabled me to correct. In strict
pronunciation they should have been sounded
vice versâ — but in those young years they
impressed me with more awe than they would
now do, read aright from Seneca or Varro — in
his own peculiar pronunciation, monosyllabically
elaborated, or Anglicized, into something like
verse verse. By an imposing manner, and the
help of these distorted syllables, he climbed
(but that was little) to the highest parochial
honours which St. Andrew's has to bestow.

He is dead ; and thus much I thought due
to his memory, both for my first orders (little
wondrous talismans ! — slight keys, and insignificant to outward sight, but opening to me
more than Arabian paradises !) and, moreover,
that by his testamentary beneficence I came into
possession of the only landed property which I
could ever call my own, — situate near the road-
way village of pleasant Puckeridge, in Hert-
fordshire. When I journeyed down to take
possession, and planted foot on my own ground,
the stately habits of the donor descended upon

me, and I strode (shall I confess the vanity ?)
with larger paces over my allotment of three
quarters of an acre, with its commodious man-
sion in the midst, with the feeling of an English
freeholder that all betwixt sky and centre was
my own.   The estate has passed into more
prudent hands, and nothing but an agrarian can
restore it.

In those days were pit-orders, — beshrew the
uncomfortable manager who abolished them ! —
with one of these we went.   I remember the
waiting at the door, — not that which is left, —
but between that and an inner door in shelter.
Oh, when shall I be such an expectant again !
— with the cry of nonpareils, an indispensable
play-house accompaniment in those days.   As
near as I can recollect, the fashionable pronunciation of the theatrical fruiteresses then was :
' Chase some oranges ; chase some numparels ;
chase a bill of the play ! ' — chase *pro* choose.
But when we got in, and I beheld the green
curtain that veiled a heaven to my imagination,
which was soon to be disclosed, — the breathless anticipations I endured !   I had seen something like it in the plate prefixed to ' Troilus and
Cressida,' in Rowe's Shakspeare, — the   tent
scene with Diomede ; and a sight of that plate
can always bring back in a measure the feeling

of that evening. The boxes at that time, full
of well-dressed women of quality, projected
over the pit; and the pilasters reaching down
were adorned with a glistening substance (I
know not what) under glass (as it seemed),
resembling — a homely fancy, but I judged it
to be — sugar-candy; yet to my raised imagination, divested of its homelier qualities, it
appeared a glorified candy! The orchestra-
lights at length rose, those 'fair Auroras!'
Once the bell sounded. It was to ring out yet
once again; and, incapable of the anticipation,
I reposed my shut eyes in a sort of resignation
upon the maternal lap. It rang the second
time. The curtain drew up, — I was not past
six years old, — and the play was ' Artaxerxes!'

I had dabbled a little in the Universal History, — the ancient part of it, — and here was
the court of Persia. It was being admitted to
a sight of the past. I took no proper interest
in the action going on, for I understood not its
import; but I heard the word ' Darius,' and I
was in the midst of Daniel. All feeling was
absorbed in vision. Gorgeous vests, gardens,
palaces, princesses, passed before me. I knew
not players. I was in Persepolis for the time,
and the burning idol of their devotion almost
converted me into a worshipper. I was awe-
struck, and believed those significations to be

something more than elemental fires. It was all enchantment and a dream; no such pleasure has since visited me but in dreams. Harlequin's invasion followed,—where, I remember, the transformation of the magistrates into reverend beldams seemed to me a piece of grave historic justice, and the tailor carrying his own head to be as sober a verity as the legend of Saint Denys.

The next play to which I was taken was the 'Lady of the Manor,'— of which, with the exception of some scenery, very faint traces are left in my memory. It was followed by a pantomime called ' Lun's Ghost,'— a satiric touch, I apprehend, upon Rich, not long since dead; but to my apprehension (too sincere for satire), Lun was as remote a piece of antiquity as Lud — the father of a line of harlequins — transmitting his dagger of lath (the wooden sceptre) through countless ages. I saw the primeval Motley come from his silent tomb in a ghastly vest of white patchwork, like the apparition of a dead rainbow. So harlequins (thought I) look when they are dead.

My third play followed in quick succession ; it was the ' Way of the World.' I think I must have sat at it as grave as a judge ; for I remember the hysteric affectations of good Lady Wishfort affected me like some solemn tragic passion.

' Robinson Crusoe ' followed, in which Crusoe, Man Friday, and the parrot were as good and authentic as in the story. The clownery and pantaloonery of these pantomimes have clean passed out of my head. I believe I no more laughed at them than at the same age I should have been disposed to laugh at the grotesque Gothic heads (seeming to me then replete with devout meaning) that gape and grin in stone around the inside of the old Round Church (my church) of the Templars.

I saw these plays in the season 1781-2, when I was from six to seven years old. After the intervention of six or seven other years (for at school all play-going was inhibited) I again entered the doors of a theatre. That old ' Artaxerxes ' evening had never done ringing in my fancy. I expected the same feelings to come again with the same occasion. But we differ from ourselves less at sixty and sixteen, than the latter does from six. In that interval what had I not lost ! At the first period I knew nothing, understood nothing, discriminated nothing. I felt all, loved all, wondered all, —

Was nourished, I could not tell how.

I had left the temple a devotee, and was returned a rationalist. The same things were there materially ; but the emblem, the reference, was gone! The green curtain was no longer a veil drawn between two worlds, the unfolding of which was to bring back past ages, to present a 'royal ghost,' but a certain quantity of green baize, which was to separate the audience for a given time from certain of their fellow-men who were to come forward and pretend those parts. The lights — the orchestra lights — came up a clumsy machinery. The first ring, and the second ring, was now but a trick of the prompter's bell, which had been, like the note of the cuckoo, a phantom of a voice, no hand seen or guessed at which ministered to its warning. The actors were men and women painted. I thought the fault was in them; but it was in myself, and the alteration which those many centuries — of six short twelvemonths — had wrought in me. Perhaps it was fortunate for me that the play of the evening was but an indifferent comedy, as it gave me time to crop some unreasonable expectations, which might have interfered with the genuine emotions with which I was soon after enabled to enter upon the first appearance to me of Mrs. Siddons in Isabella. Comparison and retrospection soon yielded to the present attraction of the scene; and the theatre became to me, upon a new stock, the most delightful of recreations.

ON SOME OF THE OLD ACTORS.

THE casual sight of an old play-bill, which I picked up the other day, — I know not by what chance it was preserved so long, — tempts me to call to mind a few of the players who make the principal figure in it. It presents the cast of parts in the 'Twelfth Night' at the old Drury Lane Theatre two and thirty years ago. There is something very touching in these old remembrances. They make us think how we *once* used to read a play-bill, — not as now, peradventure, singling out a favourite performer, and casting a negligent eye over the rest, but spelling out every name, down to the very mutes and servants of the scene ; when it was a matter of no small moment to us whether Whitfield or Packer took the part of Fabian ; when Benson and Burton and Phillimore — names of small account — had an importance beyond what we can be content to attribute now to the time's best actors. 'Orsino, by Mr. Barrymore.' What a full, Shakspearian sound it

carries! how fresh to memory arise the image
and the manner of the gentle actor! Those
who have only seen Mrs. Jordan within the
last ten or fifteen years can have no adequate
notion of her performance of such parts as
Ophelia; Helena, in ' All 's Well that Ends
Well ; ' and Viola, in this play.   Her voice had
latterly acquired a coarseness which suited
well enough with her Nells and Hoydens ; but
in those days it sank, with her steady, melting
eye, into the heart.   Her joyous parts — in
which her memory now chiefly lives — in her
youth were outdone by her plaintive ones.
There is no giving an account how she delivered
the disguised story of her love for Orsino.   It
was no set speech that she had foreseen, so as
to weave it into an harmonious period, line
necessarily following line, to make up the
music, — yet I have heard it so spoken, or
rather *read*, not without its grace and beauty, —
but when she had declared her sister's history
to be a ' blank,' and that she ' never told her
love,' there was a pause, as if the story had
ended ; and then the image of the ' worm in
the bud ' came up as a new suggestion, and
the heightened image of ' Patience ' still followed after that as by some growing (and not
mechanical) process, thought springing up after

thought, I would almost say, as they were watered by her tears. So in those fine lines —

> Write loyal cantons of contemned love —
> Halloo your name to the reverberate hills —

there was no preparation made in the foregoing image for that which was to follow. She used no rhetoric in her passion, or it was Nature's own rhetoric, most legitimate then when it seemed altogether without rule or law.

Mrs. Powel (now Mrs. Renard), then in the pride of her beauty, made an admirable Olivia. She was particularly excellent in her unbending scenes in conversation with the Clown. I have seen some Olivias — and those very sensible actresses too — who in these interlocutions have seemed to set their wits at the jester, and to vie conceits with him in downright emulation. But she used him for her sport, like what he was, to trifle a leisure sentence or two with, and then to be dismissed, and she to be the Great Lady still. She touched the imperious fantastic humour of the character with nicety. Her fine, spacious person filled the scene.

The part of Malvolio has, in my judgment, been so often misunderstood, and the *general merits* of the actor who then played it so unduly appreciated, that I shall hope for pardon if I am a little prolix upon these points.

Of all the actors who flourished in my time —
a melancholy phrase if taken aright, reader —
Bensley had most of the swell of soul, was
greatest in the delivery of heroic conceptions,
the emotions consequent upon the presentment
of a great idea to the fancy.   He had the true
poetical enthusiasm, — the rarest faculty among
players.   None that I remember possessed
even a portion of that fine madness which he
threw out in Hotspur's famous rant about glory,
or the transports of the Venetian incendiary at
the vision of the fired city.   His voice had the
dissonance, and at times the inspiriting effect, of
the trumpet.   His gait was uncouth and stiff,
but no way embarrassed by affectation ; and
the thorough-bred gentleman was uppermost in
every movement.   He seized the moment of
passion with greatest truth ; like a faithful clock,
never striking before the time, — never anticipa-
ting, or leading you to anticipate.   He was
totally destitute of trick and artifice.   He
seemed come upon the stage to do the poet's
message simply, and he did it with as genuine
fidelity as the nuncios in Homer deliver the
errands of the gods.   He let the passion or the
sentiment do its own work without prop or
bolstering.   He would have scorned to mounte-
bank it, and betrayed none of that *cleverness*

which is the bane of serious acting. For this reason, his Iago was the only endurable one which I remember to have seen. No spectator, from his action, could divine more of his artifice than Othello was supposed to do. His confessions in soliloquy alone put you in possession of the mystery. There were no by-intimations to make the audience fancy their own discernment so much greater than that of the Moor, — who commonly stands like a great helpless mark set up for mine Ancient and a quantity of barren spectators to shoot their bolts at. The Iago of Bensley did not go to work so grossly. There was a triumphant tone about the character natural to a general consciousness of power, but none of that petty vanity which chuckles and cannot contain itself upon any little successful stroke of its knavery, — as is common with your small villains and green probationers in mischief. It did not clap or crow before its time. It was not a man setting his wits at a child, and winking all the while at other children, who are mightily pleased at being let into the secret, but a consummate villain entrapping a noble nature into toils against which no discernment was available, where the manner was as fathomless as the purpose seemed dark and without motive.

The part of Malvolio in the 'Twelfth Night' was performed by Bensley with a richness and a dignity of which (to judge from some recent castings of that character) the very tradition must be worn out from the stage. No manager in those days would have dreamed of giving it to Mr. Baddely or Mr. Parsons; when Bensley was occasionally absent from the theatre, John Kemble thought it no derogation to succeed to the part. Malvolio is not essentially ludicrous. He becomes comic but by accident. He is cold, austere, repelling; but dignified, consistent, and for what appears, rather of an over-stretched morality. Maria describes him as a sort of Puritan; and he might have worn his gold chain with honour in one of our old Roundhead families in the service of a Lambert or a Lady Fairfax. But his morality and his manners are misplaced in Illyria. He is opposed to the proper *levities* of the piece, and falls in the unequal contest. Still, his pride, or his gravity (call it which you will), is inherent, and native to the man, not mock or affected, — which latter only are the fit objects to excite laughter. His quality is at the best unlovely, but neither buffoon nor contemptible. His bearing is lofty,— a little above his station, but probably not much above his deserts. We see no reason why he should not have been brave, honourable, accomplished. His careless committal of the ring to the ground (which he was commissioned to restore to Cesario) bespeaks a generosity of birth and feeling. His dialect on all occasions is that of a gentleman and a man of education. We must not confound him with the eternal old, low steward of comedy. He is master of the household to a great princess,—a dignity probably conferred upon him for other respects than age or length of service. Olivia, at the first indication of his supposed madness, declares that she ' would not have him miscarry for half of her dowry.' Does this look as if the character was meant to appear little, or insignificant ? Once, indeed, she accuses him to his face—of what ? Of being ' sick of self-love ; ' but with a gentleness and considerateness which could not have been if she had not thought that this particular infirmity shaded some virtues. His rebuke to the knight and his sottish revellers is sensible and spirited ; and when we take into consideration the unprotected condition of his mistress, and the strict regard with which her state of real or dissembled mourning would draw the eyes of the world upon her house-affairs, Malvolio might feel the honour of the family in some sort in his

D

keeping, — as it appears not that Olivia had any
more brothers or kinsmen to look to it ; for
Sir Toby had dropped all such nice respects at
the buttery-hatch. That Malvolio was meant
to be represented as possessing estimable qualities, the expression of the Duke, in his anxiety
to have him reconciled, almost infers : ' Pursue
him, and entreat him to a peace.' Even in his
abused state of chains and darkness, a sort of
greatness seems never to desert him. He
argues highly and well with the supposed Sir
Topas, and philosophizes gallantly upon his
straw.[1] There must have been some shadow
of worth about the man ; he must have been
something more than a mere vapour — a thing
of straw, or Jack in office — before Fabian and
Maria could have ventured sending him upon a
courting-errand to Olivia. There was some
consonancy (as he would say) in the undertak-
ing, or the jest would have been too bold even
for that house of misrule.

---

[1] *Clown.* What is the opinion of Pythagoras concern-
         ing wild fowl ?

Mal.   That the soul of our grandam might haply
         inhabit a bird.

Clown. What thinkest thou of his opinion ?

Mal.   I think nobly of the soul, and no way approve
         of his opinion.

Bensley, accordingly, threw over the part an air of Spanish loftiness. He looked, spake, and moved like an old Castilian. He was starch, spruce, opinionated, but his superstructure of pride seemed bottomed upon a sense of worth ; there was something in it beyond the coxcomb. It was big and swelling, but you could not be sure that it was hollow. You might wish to see it taken down, but you felt that it was upon an elevation. He was magnificent from the outset ; but when the decent sobrieties of the character began to give way, and the poison of self-love, in his conceit of the Countess's affection, gradually to work, you would have thought that the hero of La Mancha in person stood before you. How he went smiling to himself ; with what ineffable carelessness would he twirl his gold chain ; what a dream it was ! You were infected with the illusion, and did not wish that it should be removed ; you had no room for laughter ! If an unseasonable reflection of morality obtruded itself, it was a deep sense of the pitiable infirmity of man's nature, that can lay him open to such frenzies ; but, in truth, you rather admired than pitied the lunacy while it lasted, — you felt that an hour of such mistake was worth an age with the eyes open. Who would not wish to live but for a day in the con-

ceit of such a lady's love as Olivia ?   Why, the
Duke would have given his principality but for a
quarter of a minute, sleeping or waking, to have
been so deluded.   The man seemed to tread
upon air, to taste manna, to walk with his head
in the clouds, to mate Hyperion.   Oh, shake
not the castles of his pride ; endure yet for a
season, bright moments of confidence ; ' stand
still, ye watches of the element,' that Malvolio
may be still in fancy fair Olivia's lord !   But
fate and retribution say no ; I hear the mis-
chievous titter of Maria, the witty taunts of
Sir Toby, the still more insupportable triumph of the foolish knight.   The counterfeit Sir
Topas is unmasked, and ' thus the whirligig
of time,' as the true Clown hath it, ' brings in
his revenges.'   I confess that I never saw the
catastrophe of this character, while Bensley
played it, without a kind of tragic interest.
There was good foolery too.   Few now
remember Dodd.   What an Aguecheek the
stage lost in him !   Lovegrove, who came
nearest to the old actors, revived the character
some few seasons ago, and made it sufficiently
grotesque ; but Dodd was *it*, as it came out of
Nature's hands.   It might be said to remain *in
puris naturalibus*.   In expressing slowness of apprehension, this actor surpassed all others.   You

could see the first dawn of an idea stealing slowly over his countenance, climbing up by little and little, with a painful process, till it cleared up at last to the fulness of a twilight conception, — its highest meridian. He seemed to keep back his intellect, as some have had the power to retard their pulsation. The balloon takes less time in filling than it took to cover the expansion of his broad, moony face over all its quarters with expression. A glimmer of understanding would appear in a corner of his eye, and for lack of fuel go out again. A part of his forehead would catch a little intelligence, and be a long time in communicating it to the remainder.

I am ill at dates, but I think it is now better than five and twenty years ago, that, walking in the gardens of Gray's Inn (they were then far finer than they are now, — the accursed Verulam Buildings had not encroached upon all the east side of them, cutting out delicate green crankles, and shouldering away one or two of the stately alcoves of the terrace ; the survivor stands gaping and relationless, as if it remembered its brother, — they are still the best gardens of any of the Inns of Court, my beloved Temple not forgotten, have the gravest character, their aspect being altogether reverend and law-breathing, Bacon has left the impress of his

foot upon their gravel-walks), — taking my afternoon solace on a summer day upon the aforesaid
terrace, a comely, sad personage came towards
me, whom, from his grave air and deportment, I
judged to be one of the old Benchers of the Inn.
He had a serious, thoughtful forehead, and
seemed to be in meditations of mortality. As
I have an instinctive awe of old Benchers, I
was passing him with that sort of sub-indicative
token of respect which one is apt to demonstrate
towards a venerable stranger, and which rather
denotes an inclination to greet him than any
positive motion of the body to that effect, — a
species of humility and will-worship which, I
observe, nine times out of ten rather puzzles
than pleases the person it is offered to, — when
the face, turning full upon me, strangely identi-
fied itself with that of Dodd. Upon close in-
spection I was not mistaken. But could this
sad, thoughtful countenance be the same vacant
face of folly which I had hailed so often under
circumstances of gaiety ; which I had never seen
without a smile, or recognized but as the usher
of mirth ; that looked out so formally flat in
Foppington, so frothily pert in Tattle, so impo-
tently busy in Backbite, so blankly divested of
all meaning, or resolutely expressive of none,
in Acres, in Fribble, and a thousand agreeable

impertinences? Was this the face — full of
thought and carefulness — that had so often divested itself at will of every trace of either to
give me diversion, to clear my cloudy face for
two or three hours at least of its furrows? Was
this the face — manly, sober, intelligent — which
I had so often despised, made mocks at, made
merry with? The remembrance of the freedoms
which I had taken with it came upon me with
a reproach of insult. I could have asked it
pardon. I thought it looked upon me with a
sense of injury. There is something strange as
well as sad in seeing actors — your pleasant
fellows particularly — subjected to and suffering
the common lot ; their fortunes, their casual-
ties, their deaths, seem to belong to the scene,
their actions to be amenable to poetic justice
only. We can hardly connect them with more
awful responsibilities. The death of this fine
actor took place shortly after this meeting. He
had quitted the stage some months, and, as I
learned afterwards, had been in the habit of
resorting daily to these gardens, almost to
the day of his decease. In these serious
walks, probably, he was divesting himself of
many scenic and some real vanities, weaning
himself from the frivolities of the lesser and
the greater theatre, doing gentle penance for a

life of no very reprehensible fooleries, taking
off by degrees the buffoon mask which he might
feel he had worn too long, and rehearsing for
a more solemn cast of part. Dying, he 'put
on the weeds of Dominic.'[1]

If few can remember Dodd, many yet living
will not easily forget the pleasant creature who
in those days enacted the part of the Clown to
Dodd's Sir Andrew. Richard, or rather Dicky,
Suett — for so in his lifetime he delighted to be
called, and time hath ratified the appellation —
lieth buried on the north side of the cemetery of
Holy Paul, to whose service his nonage and
tender years were dedicated. There are who do
yet remember him at that period, — his pipe clear
and harmonious. He would often speak of his
chorister days, when he was 'cherub Dicky.'

[1] Dodd was a man of reading, and left at his death a
choice collection of old English literature. I should
judge him to have been a man of wit. I know one instance of an impromptu which no length of study could
have bettered. My merry friend Jem White had seen
him one evening in Aguecheek, and recognizing Dodd the
next day in Fleet Street, was irresistibly impelled to take
off his hat and salute him, as the identical knight of the
preceding evening, with a 'Save you, *Sir Andrew.*'
Dodd, not at all disconcerted at this unusual address
from a stranger. with a courteous, half-rebuking wave of
the hand, put him off with an '*Away, Fool.*'

What clipped his wings, or made it expedient that he should exchange the holy for the profane state ; whether he had lost his good voice (his best recommendation to that office), like Sir John, 'with hallooing and singing of anthems ; ' or whether he was adjudged to lack something, even in those early years, of the gravity indispensable to an occupation which professeth to 'commerce with the skies,' — I could never rightly learn ; but we find him, after the probation of a twelvemonth or so, reverting to a secular condition and become one of us.

I think he was not altogether of that timber out of which cathedral seats and sounding-boards are hewed. But if a glad heart — kind, and therefore glad — be any part of sanctity, then might the robe of Motley, with which he invested himself with so much humility after his deprivation, and which he wore so long with so much blameless satisfaction to himself and to the public, be accepted for a surplice, — his white stole and *albe*.

The first-fruits of his secularization was an engagement upon the boards of Old Drury, at which theatre he commenced, as I have been told, with adopting the manner of Parsons in old men's characters. At the period in which most of us knew him, he was no more an imitator than he was in any true sense himself imitable.

He was the Robin Goodfellow of the stage. He came in to trouble all things with a welcome perplexity, himself no whit troubled for the matter. He was known, like Puck, by his note, *Ha! Ha! Ha!* sometimes deepening to *Ho! Ho! Ho!* with an irresistible accession, derived, perhaps, remotely from his ecclesiastical education, foreign to his prototype, of *O La!* Thousands of hearts yet respond to the chuckling *O La!* of Dicky Suett, brought back to their remembrance by the faithful transcript of his friend Mathews's mimicry. The 'force of nature could no further go.' He drolled upon the stock of these two syllables richer than the cuckoo.

Care, that troubles all the world, was forgotten in his composition. Had he had but two grains (nay, half a grain) of it, he could never have supported himself upon those two spider's strings which served him (in the latter part of his unmixed existence) as legs. A doubt or a scruple must have made him totter, a sigh have puffed him down ; the weight of a frown had staggered him, a wrinkle made him lose his balance. But on he went, scrambling upon those airy stilts of his, with Robin Goodfellow,

' thorough brake, thorough brier,' reckless of a scratched face or a torn doublet.

Shakspeare foresaw him when he framed his fools and jesters. They have all the true Suett stamp, — a loose and shambling gait, a slippery tongue (this last the ready midwife to a without-pain-delivered jest) ; in words light as air, venting truths deep as the centre ; with idlest rhymes tagging conceit when busiest, singing with Lear in the tempest, or Sir Toby at the buttery-hatch.

Jack Bannister and he had the fortune to be more of personal favourites with the town than any actors before or after. The difference, I take it, was this : Jack was more *beloved* for his sweet, good-natured, moral pretensions. Dicky was more *liked* for his sweet, good-natured no pretensions at all. Your whole conscience stirred with Bannister's performance of Walter in the ' Children in the Wood ' ; but Dicky seemed like a thing, as Shakspeare says of Love, too young to know what conscience is. He put us into Vesta's days. Evil fled before him, — not as from Jack, as from an antagonist, but because it could not touch him, any more than a cannon-ball a fly. He was delivered from the burthen of that death ; and when Death came himself — not in metaphor — to fetch Dicky, it is recorded of him by Robert Palmer,

who kindly watched his exit, that he received
the last stroke, neither varying his accustomed
tranquillity nor tune, with the simple exclama-
tion, worthy to have been recorded in his epi-
taph, *O La ! O La ! Bobby·!*

The elder Palmer (of stage-trading celebrity)
commonly played Sir Toby in those days ; but
there is a solidity of wit in the jests of that half-
Falstaff which he did not quite fill out.   He
was as much too showy as Moody (who sometimes took the part) was dry and sottish.   In
sock or buskin there was an air of swagger-
ing gentility about Jack Palmer.   He was a
gentleman with a slight infusion of *the footman.*
His brother Bob (of recenter memory), who
was his shadow in everything while he lived,
and dwindled into less than a shadow afterwards, was a *gentleman* with a little stronger
infusion of the *latter ingredient;* that was all.
It is amazing how a little of the more or less
makes a difference in these things.   When you
saw Bobby in the ' Duke's Servant,'[1] you said,
' What a pity such a pretty fellow was only a
servant ! '   When you saw Jack figuring in
Captain Absolute, you thought you could trace
his promotion to some lady of quality who
fancied the handsome fellow in his topknot,

[1] High Life Below Stairs.

and had bought him a commission. Therefore Jack in Dick Amlet was insuperable.

Jack had two voices, both plausible, hypocritical, and insinuating, but his secondary, or supplemental, voice still more decisively histrionic than his common one. It was reserved for the spectator; and the *dramatis personæ* were supposed to know nothing at all about it. The *lies* of Young Wilding, and the *sentiments* in Joseph Surface, were thus marked out in a sort of italics to the audience. This secret correspondence with the company before the curtain (which is the bane and death of tragedy) has an extremely happy effect in some kinds of comedy, in the more highly artificial comedy of Congreve or of Sheridan especially, where the absolute sense of reality (so indispensable to scenes of interest) is not required, or would rather interfere to diminish your pleasure. The fact is, you do not believe in such characters as Surface — the villain of artificial comedy — even while you read or see them. If you did, they would shock, and not divert you. When Ben, in 'Love for Love,' returns from sea, the following exquisite dialogue occurs at his first meeting with his father : —

Sir Sampson. Thou hast been many a weary league, Ben, since I saw thee.

Ben. Ey, ey, been. Been far enough, an that be all. — Well, father, and how do all at home? How does brother Dick and brother Val?

Sir Sampson. Dick! body o' me, Dick has been dead these two years. I writ you word when you were at Leghorn.

Ben. Mess, that's true; marry, I had forgot. Dick's dead, as you say. Well, and how?— I have a many questions to ask you.

Here is an instance of insensibility which in real life would be revolting, or rather in real life could not have co-existed with the warm-hearted temperament of the character. But when you read it in the spirit with which such playful selections and specious combinations rather than strict *metaphrases* of nature should be taken, or when you saw Bannister play it, it neither did, nor does, wound the moral sense at all. For what is Ben — the pleasant sailor which Bannister gives us — but a piece of satire, a creation of Congreve's fancy, a dreamy combination of all the accidents of a sailor's character, — his contempt of money, his credulity to women, with that necessary estrangement from home which it is just within the verge of credibility to suppose *might* produce such an hallucination as is here described. We never think the worse of Ben for it, or feel it as a stain upon his character.

But when an actor comes, and instead of the delightful phantom — the creature dear to half-belief — which Bannister exhibited, displays before our eyes a downright concretion of a Wapping sailor, a jolly, warm-hearted Jack Tar, and nothing else ; when, instead of investing it with a delicious confusedness of the head, and a veering, undirected goodness of purpose, he gives to it a downright daylight understanding and a full consciousness of its actions, thrusting forward the sensibilities of the character with a pretence as if it stood upon nothing else, and was to be judged by them alone, — we feel the discord of the thing ; the scene is disturbed ; a real man has got in among the *dramatis personæ*, and puts them out. We want the sailor turned out. We feel that his true place is not behind the curtain, but in the first or second gallery.

THE OLD ACTORS.

I DO not know a more mortifying thing than to be conscious of a foregone delight, with a total oblivion of the person and manner which conveyed it. In dreams I often stretch and strain after the countenance of Edwin, whom I once saw in ' Peeping Tom.' I cannot catch a feature of him. He is no more to me than Nokes or Pinkethman. Parsons, and still more Dodd, were near being lost to me till I was refreshed with their portraits (fine treat) the other day at Mr. Matthews's gallery at Highgate, which, with the exception of the Hogarth pictures a few years since exhibited in Pall-Mall, was the most delightful collection I ever gained admission to. There hang the players, in their single persons and in grouped scenes, from the Restoration, — Bettertons, Booths, Garricks, — justifying the prejudices which we entertain for them ; the Bracegirdles, the Mountforts, and the Oldfields, fresh as Cibber has described them ; the Woffington (a true Hogarth) upon a couch, dallying and dangerous ; the screen-scene in Brinsley's famous comedy, with Smith and Mrs. Abington, whom I have not seen ; and the rest, whom, having seen, I see still there. There is Henderson, unrivalled in Comus, whom I saw at second-hand in the elder Harley ; Harley, the rival of Holman, in Horatio ; Holman, with the bright, glittering teeth, in Lothario, and the deep paviour's sighs in Romeo, the jolliest person ('our son is fat') of any Hamlet I have yet seen, with the most laudable attempts (for a personable man) at looking melancholy ; and Pope, the abdicated monarch of tragedy and comedy, in Harry the Eighth ; and Lord Townley. There hang the two Aickins, brethren in mediocrity ; Wroughton, who in Kitely seemed to have forgotten that in prouder days he had personated Alexander ; the specious form of John Palmer, with the special effrontery of Bobby ; Bensley, with the trumpet tongue ; and little Quick (the retired Dioclesian of Islington), with his squeak like a Bart'lemew fiddle. There are fixed, cold as in life, the immovable features of Moody, who, afraid of o'erstepping Nature, sometimes stopped short of her ; and the rest·

E

less fidgetiness of Lewis, who, with no such
fears, not seldom leaped o' the other side.
There hang Farren and Whitfield, and Burton
and Phillimore, — names of small account in
those times, but which, remembered now, or
casually recalled by the sight of an old playbill,
with their associated recordations, can 'drown
an eye unused to flow.' There too hangs, not
far removed from them in death, the graceful
plainness of the first Mrs. Pope, with a voice
unstrung by age, but which in her better days
must have competed with the silver tones of
Barry himself, so enchanting in decay do I
remember it, — of all her lady parts, exceeding
herself in the 'Lady Quakeress' (there earth
touched heaven) of O'Keefe, when she played
it to the 'merry cousin' of Lewis ; and Mrs.
Mattocks, the sensiblest of viragos ; and Miss
Pope, a gentlewoman ever, to the verge of
ungentility, with Churchill's compliment still
burnishing upon her gay honeycomb lips.
There are the two Bannisters and Sedgwick,
and Kelly and Dignum (Diggy), and the by-
gone features of Mrs. Ward, matchless in Lady
Loverule ; and the collective majesty of the
whole Kemble family ; and (Shakspeare's
woman) Dora Jordan, who by her *two antics,*

in former and in latter days, have chiefly be-guiled us of our griefs, and whose portraits we shall strive to recall for the sympathy of those who may not have had the benefit of viewing the matchless Highgate collection.

ON THE ACTING OF MUNDEN.

NOT many nights ago I had come home from seeing this extraordinary performer in *Cockletop;* and when I retired to my pillow his whimsical image still stuck by me in a manner as to threaten sleep.   In vain I tried to divest myself of it by conjuring up the most opposite associations.   I resolved to be serious. I raised up the gravest topics of life, private misery, public calamity.   All would not do ;

> There the antic sat,
> Mocking our state, —

his queer visnomy, his bewildering costume, all the strange things which he had raked together, his serpentine rod swagging about in his pocket, Cleopatra's tear, and the rest of his relics, O'Keefe's wild farce, and *his* wilder commentary, till the passion of laughter, like grief in excess, relieved itself by its own weight, inviting the sleep which in the first instance it had driven away.

But I was not to escape so easily. No sooner did I fall into slumbers than the same image, only more perplexing, assailed me in the shape of dreams. Not one Munden, but five hundred, were dancing before me, like the faces which, whether you will or no, come when you have been taking opium, — all the strange combinations which this strangest of all strange mortals ever shot his proper countenance into, from the day he came commissioned to dry up the tears of the town for the loss of the now almost forgotten Edwin. Oh, for the power of the pencil to have fixed them when I awoke ! A season or two since there was exhibited a Hogarth gallery. I do not see why there should not be a Munden gallery. In richness and variety, the latter would not fall far short of the former.

There is one face of Farley, one face of Knight, one (but what a one it is !) of Liston ; but Munden has none that you can properly pin down and call *his*. When you think he has exhausted his battery of looks, in unaccountable warfare with your gravity, suddenly he sprouts out an entirely new set of features, like Hydra. He is not one, but legion ; not so much a comedian as a company. If his name could be multiplied like his countenance, it might fill a playbill. He, and he alone, literally *makes faces;* applied to any other person, the phrase is a mere figure, denoting certain modifications of the human countenance. Out of some invisible wardrobe he dips for faces, as his friend Suett used for wigs, and fetches them out as easily. I should not be surprised to see him some day put out the head of a river-horse, or come forth a pewit or lapwing, some feathered metamorphosis.

I have seen this gifted actor in Sir Christopher Curry, in old Dornton, diffuse a glow of sentiment which has made the pulse of a crowded theatre beat like that of one man, when he has come in aid of the pulpit, doing good to the moral heart of a people. I have seen some faint approaches to this sort of excellence in other players. But in the grand grotesque of farce, Munden stands out as single and unaccompanied as Hogarth. Hogarth, strange to tell, had no followers. The school of Munden began and must end with himself.

Can any man *wonder* like he does? can any man *see ghosts* like he does? or *fight with his own shadow*, 'SESSA,' as he does in that strangely-neglected thing, the 'Cobbler of Preston,' where his alterations from the Cobbler

to the Magnifico, and from the Magnifico to
the Cobbler, keep the brain of the spectator
in as wild a ferment as if some Arabian Night
were being acted before him? Who like him
can throw, or ever attempted to throw, a preternatural interest over the commonest daily
life objects? A table or a joint stool, in his
conception, rises into a dignity equivalent to
Cassiopeia's chair; it is invested with con-
stellatory importance. You could not speak of
it with more deference if it were mounted into
the firmament. A beggar in the hands of
Michael Angelo, says Fuseli, rose the Patriarch
of Poverty. So the gusto of Munden anti-
quates and ennobles what it touches. His pots
and his ladles are as grand and primal as the
seething-pots and hooks seen in old prophetic
vision. A tub of butter, contemplated by him,
amounts to a Platonic idea. He understands
a leg of mutton in its quiddity. He stands
wondering, amid the commonplace materials of
life, like primeval man with the sun and stars
about him.

MUNDEN'S FAREWELL.

THE regular playgoers ought to put on mourning, for the king of broad comedy is dead to the drama. Alas ! Munden is no more ! —give sorrow vent. He may yet walk the town, pace the pavement in a seeming existence, eat, drink, and nod to his friends in all the affectation of life ; but Munden, *the* Munden, Munden with the bunch of countenances, the bouquet of faces, is gone forever from the lamps, and as far as comedy is concerned, is as dead as Garrick ! When an actor retires (we will put the *suicide* as mildly as possible), how many worthy persons perish with him ! With Munden Sir Peter Teazle must experience a shock ; Sir Robert Bramble gives up the ghost ; Crack ceases to breathe. Without Munden what becomes of Dozey ? Where shall we seek Jemmy Jumps ? Nipperkin and a thousand of such admirable fooleries fall to nothing, and the departure, therefore, of such an actor as Munden is a dramatic calamity. On the night that this inestimable humorist took farewell of the public, he also took his benefit, — a benefit in which the public assuredly did not participate. The play was Coleman's ' Poor Gentleman,' with Tom Dibdin's farce of ' Past Ten o'Clock.' Reader, we all know Munden in Sir Robert Bramble and old tobacco-complexioned Dozey; we all have seen the old hearty baronet in his light sky-blue coat and genteel cocked hat, and we have all seen the weather-beaten old pensioner, dear old Dozey, tacking about the stage in that intense blue sea livery, drunk as heart could wish, and right valorous in memory. On this night Munden seemed, like the Gladiator, ' to rally life's whole energies to die ; ' and as we were present at this great display of his powers, and as this will be the last opportunity that will ever be afforded us to speak of this admirable performer, we shall ' consecrate,' as old John Buncle says, ' a paragraph to him.'

The house was full. *Full !* — pshaw ! that 's an empty word ! The house was stuffed, crammed with people, — crammed from the swing-door of the pit to the back-seat in the banished *one shilling*. A quart of audience may be said (vintner-like, may it be said) to have been squeezed into a pint of theatre. Every hearty playgoing Londoner who remembered Munden years agone mustered up his courage and his money for this benefit, and middle-aged people were therefore by no means scarce. The comedy chosen for the occasion is one that travels a long way without a guard, — it is not until the third or fourth act, we think, that Sir Robert Bramble appears on the stage. When he entered, his reception was earnest, noisy, outrageous ; waving of hats and handkerchiefs, deafening shouts, clamorous beating of sticks, — all the various ways in which the heart is accustomed to manifest its joy, — were had recourse to on this occasion. Mrs. Bamfield worked away with a sixpenny fan till she scudded only under bare poles. Mr. Whittington wore out the ferule of a new nine-and-sixpenny umbrella. Gratitude did great damage on the joyful occasion.

The old performer, the veteran, as he appropriately called himself in the farewell speech, was plainly overcome ; he pressed his hands together, he planted one solidly on his breast, he bowed, he sidled, he cried. When the noise subsided (which it invariably does at last), the comedy proceeded, and Munden gave an admirable picture of the rich, eccentric, charitable old bachelor baronet who goes about with Humphrey Dobbin at his heels and philanthropy in his heart. How crustily and yet how kindly he takes Humphrey's contradictions. How readily he puts himself into an attitude for arguing. How tenderly he gives a loose to his heart on the apprehension of Frederick's duel. In truth he played Sir Robert in his very ripest manner ; and it was impossible not to feel in the very midst of pleasure regret that Munden should then be before us for the last time.

In the farce he became richer and richer. Old Dozey is a plant from Greenwich. The bronzed face and neck to match, the long curtain of a coat, the straggling white hair, the propensity, the determined attachment to grog, are all from Greenwich. Munden as Dozey seems never to have been out of action, sun, and drink. He looks (alas ! he *looked*) fireproof. His face and throat were dried like a raisin, and his legs walked under the rum-and-water with all the indecision which that inestimable beverage usually inspires. It is truly tacking, not walking. He *steers* at a table, and the tide of grog now and then bears him off the point. On this night he seemed to us to be doomed to fall in action ; and we therefore looked at him, as some of the ' Victory's ' crew are said to have gazed upon Nelson, with a consciousness that his ardour and his uniform were

worn for the last time. In the scene where
Dozey describes a sea-fight, the actor never
was greater, and he seemed the personification
of an old seventy-four !   His coat hung like a
flag at his poop.   His phiz was not a whit less
highly coloured than one of those lustrous vis-
ages which generally superintend the head of a
ship.   There was something cumbrous, inde-
cisive, and awful in his veerings.   Once afloat,
it appeared impossible for him to come to his
moorings ; once at anchor, it did not seem an
easy thing to get him under weigh.

The time, however, came for the fall of the
curtain and for the fall of Munden.   The farce
of the night was finished.   The farce of the
long forty years' play was over.   He stepped
forward, not as Dozey, but as Munden, and we
heard him address us from the stage for the last
time.   He trusted — unwisely, we think — to a
written paper.   He *read* of ' heartfelt recollections ' and ' indelible impressions.'   He stam-
mered and he pressed his heart, and put on his
spectacles, and blundered his written gratitudes,
and wiped his eyes, and bowed and stood, and
at last staggered away forever.   The plan of
his farewell was bad, but the long life of excellence which really made his farewell pathetic
overcame all defects, and the people and Joe

Munden parted like lovers. Well! Farewell to the Rich Old Heart. May thy retirement be as full of repose as thy public life was full of excellence. We must all have our farewell benefits in our turn.

THE DEATH OF MUNDEN.

YOUR communication to me of the death of Munden made me weep. Now, sir, I am not of the melting mood ; but in these serious times the loss of half the world's fun is no trivial deprivation. It was my loss (or *gain* shall I call it ?), in the early time of my playgoing, to have missed all Munden's acting. There was only he and Lewis at Covent Garden, while Drury Lane was exuberant with Parsons, Dodd, etc., — such a comic company as, I suppose, the stage never showed. Thence, in the evening of my life, I had Munden all to myself, more mellowed, richer, perhaps, than ever. I cannot say what his change of faces produced in me. It was not acting. He was not one of my 'old actors.' It might be better. His power was extravagant. I saw him one evening in three drunken characters. Three farces were played. One part was Dozey, — I forget the rest ; but they were so discriminated that a stranger might have seen them all, and not have dreamed that he was seeing the same actor. I am jealous for the actors who pleased my youth. He was not a Parsons or a Dodd, but he was more wonderful. He seemed as if he could *do* anything. He was not an actor, but something *better*, if you please. Shall I instance Old Foresight in ' Love for Love,' in which Parsons was at once the old man, the astrologer, etc.? Munden dropped the old man, the doater, — which makes the character, — but he substituted for it a moon-struck character, a perfect abstraction from this earth, that looked as if he had newly come down from the planets. Now, *that* is not what I call *acting*. It might be better. He was imaginative ; he could impress upon an audience an *idea*, — the low one, perhaps, of a leg of mutton and turnips ; but such was the grandeur and singleness of his expressions that that single expression would convey to all his auditory a notion of all the pleasures they had all received from all the legs of mutton *and turnips* they had ever eaten in their lives. Now, this is not *acting*, nor do I set down Munden amongst my old actors. He was only a wonderful man, exerting his vivid impressions through the agency of the stage. In one only thing did I see him *act*, — that is, support a character ; it was in a wretched

farce called 'Johnny Gilpin,' for Dowton's
benefit, in which he did a Cockney.   The
thing ran but one night ; but when I say that
Lubin's Log was nothing to it, I say little, — it
was transcendent.   And here let me say of
actors, — *envious* actors, — that of *Munden*, Liston was used to speak almost with the enthusiasm due to the dead, in terms of such allowed
superiority to every actor on the stage, and this
at a time when Munden was gone by in the
world's estimation, that it convinced me that
artists (in which term I include poets, painters,
etc.) are not so envious as the world think.   I
have little time, and therefore enclose a criticism
on Munden's Old Dozey and his general acting
by a gentleman who attends less to these things
than formerly, but whose criticism I think
masterly.

AUTOBIOGRAPHY OF MR. MUNDEN.

HARK'EE, Mr. Editor, a word in your ear. They tell me you are going to put me in print, — in print, sir; to publish my life. What is my life to you, sir? What is it to you whether I ever lived at all? My life is a very good life, sir. I am insured in the Pelican, sir. I am threescore years and six, — six, mark me, sir; but I can play Polonius, which, I believe, few of your corre — correspondents can do, sir. I suspect tricks, sir; I smell a rat; I do, I do. You would cog the die upon us; you would, you would, sir. But I will forestall you, sir. You would be deriving me from William the Conqueror, with a murrain to you. It is no such a thing, sir. The town shall know better, sir. They begin to smoke your flams, sir. Mr. Liston may be born where he pleases, sir; but I will not be born at Lup — Lupton Magna for anybody's pleasure, sir. My son and I have looked over the great map of Kent together, and we can find no such

F

place as you would palm upon us, sir, — palm
upon us, I say. Neither Magna nor Parva, as my
son says; and he knows Latin, sir, — Latin. If
you write my life true, sir, you must set down
that I, Joseph Munden, comedian, came into the
world upon All-hallows day, Anno Domini 1759
— 1759; no sooner nor later, sir; and I saw
the first light — the first light, remember, sir — at
Stoke Pogis — Stoke Pogis, *comitatu* Bucks,
and not at Lup — Lup Magna, which I believe
to be no better than moonshine, — moonshine;
do you mark me, sir? I wonder you can put
such flim-flams upon us, sir; I do, I do. It
does not become you, sir; I say it, — I say it.
And my father was an honest tradesman, sir;
he dealt in malt and hops, sir; and was a cor-
poration-man, sir; and of the Church of England, sir, and no Presbyterian, nor Ana — anabaptist, sir; however you may be disposed to
make honest people believe to the contrary,
sir. Your bams are found out, sir. The town
will be your stale-puts no longer, sir; and you
must not send us jolly fellows, sir, — we that
are comedians, sir, — you must not send us into
groves and char — charnwoods a-moping, sir.
Neither charns, nor charnel-houses, sir. It
is not our constitution, sir; I tell it you, —
I tell it you. I was a droll dog from my

cradle. I came into the world tittering, and
the midwife tittered, and the gossips spilt their
caudle with tittering ; and when I was brought
to the font, the parson could not christen me
for tittering. So I was never more than half
baptized. And when I was little Joey, I made
'em all titter ; there was not a melancholy face
to be seen in Pogis. Pure nature, sir. I was
born a comedian. Old Screwup, the under-
taker, could tell you, sir, if he were living.
Why, I was obliged to be locked up every time
there was to be a funeral at Pogis. I was — I
was, sir ! I used to *grimace* at the mutes, as
he called it, and put 'em out with my mops and
my mows, till they could n't stand at a door for
me. And when I was locked up, with nothing
but a cat in my company, I followed my bent
with trying to make her laugh ; and sometimes
she would, and sometimes she would not.
And my schoolmaster could make nothing of
me. I had only to thrust my tongue in my
cheek, — in my cheek, sir, — and the rod dropped
from his fingers ; and so my education was
limited, sir. And I grew up a young fellow,
and it was thought convenient to enter me upon
some course of life that should make me serious ;
but it would n't do, sir. And I was articled to
a drysalter. My father gave forty pounds pre-.

mium with me, sir. I can show the ident —
dent — dentures, sir. But I was born to be a
comedian, sir; so I ran away, and listed with
the players, sir. And I topped my parts at Amer-
sham and Gerrard's Cross, and played my own
father to his face, in his own town of Pogis, in
the part of Gripe, when I was not full seventeen
years of age; and he did not know me again,
but he knew me afterwards; and then he
laughed, and I laughed, and, what is better,
the drysalter laughed, and gave me up my
articles for the joke's sake : so that I came into
court afterwards with clean hands — with clean
hands — do you see, sir ?

[Here the manuscript becomes illegible for
two or three sheets onwards, which we presume
to be occasioned by the absence of Mr. Munden, Jun., who clearly transcribed it for the
press thus far. The rest (with the exception of
the concluding paragraph, which is seemingly
resumed in the first handwriting) appears to
contain a confused account of some lawsuit
in which the elder Munden was engaged, with
a circumstantial history of the proceedings of a
case of breach of promise of marriage, made to
or by (we cannot pick out which) Jemima
Munden, spinster, — probably the comedian's

cousin, for it does not appear he had any
sister ; with a few dates, rather better preserved, of this great actor's engagements, — as
' Cheltenham [spelt Cheltnam], 1776 ; ' ' Bath,
1779 ;' ' London, 1789 ;' together with stage
anecdotes of Messrs. Edwin, Wilson, Lee,
Lewis, etc. ; over which we have strained our
eyes to no purpose, in the hope of presenting
something amusing to the public.   Towards the
end, the manuscript brightens up a little, as we
said, and concludes in the following manner :]

— stood before them for six and thirty years
[we suspect that Mr. Munden is here speaking
of his final leave-taking of the stage], and to be
dismissed at last.   But I was heart-whole to
the last, sir.   What though a few drops did
course themselves down the old veteran's
cheeks, — who could help it, sir ?   I was a giant
that night, sir ; and could have played fifty
parts, each as arduous as Dozey.   My faculties
were never better, sir.   But I was to be laid
upon the shelf.   It did not suit the public to
laugh with their old servant any longer, sir.
[Here some moisture has blotted a sentence or
two.]   But I can play Polonius still, sir ; I can,
I can.   Your servant, sir,

JOSEPH MUNDEN.

BIOGRAPHICAL MEMOIR OF MR. LISTON.

THE subject of our Memoir is lineally descended from Johan de L'Estonne (see
'Domesday Book,' where he is so written),
who came in with the Conqueror, and had
lands awarded him at Lupton Magna, in Kent.
His particular merits or services, Fabian, whose
authority I chiefly follow, has forgotten, or perhaps thought it immaterial, to specify. Fuller
thinks that he was standard-bearer to Hugo de
Agmondesham, a powerful Norman baron who
was slain by the hand of Harold himself at the
fatal battle of Hastings. Be this as it may, we
find a family of that name flourishing some centuries later in that county. John Delliston,
knight, was High Sheriff for Kent, according to
Fabian, *quinto Henrici Sexti;* and we trace the
lineal branch flourishing downwards, — the or-
thography varying, according to the unsettled
usage of the times, from Delleston to Leston or
Liston, between which it seems to have alter-
nated, till, in the latter end of the reign of

James I., it finally settled into the determinate and pleasing dissyllabic arrangement which it still retains. Aminadab Liston, the eldest male representative of the family of that day, was of the strictest order of Puritans. Mr. Foss, of Pall-Mall, has obligingly communicated to me an undoubted tract of his, which bears the initials only, A. L., and is entitled, ' The Grinning Glass, or Actor's Mirrour ; wherein the vituperative Visnomy of Vicious Players for the Scene is as virtuously reflected back upon their mimetic Monstrosities as it has viciously (hitherto) vitiated with its vile Vanities her Votarists.' A strange title, but bearing the impress of those absurdities with which the title-pages of that pamphlet-spawning age abounded. The work bears date 1617. It preceded the ' Histriomastix ' by fifteen years ; and as it went before it in time, so it comes not far short of it in virulence. It is amusing to find an ancestor of Liston's thus bespattering the players at the commencement of the seven- teenth century : —

' Thinketh He ' (the actor), ' with his cos- tive countenances, to wry a sorrowing soul out of her anguish, or by defacing the divine de- notement of destinate dignity (daignely described in the face humane and no other) to reinstamp

the Paradice-plotted similitude with a novel and
naughty approximation (not in the first inten-
tion) to those abhorred and ugly God-forbidden
correspondences, with flouting Apes' jeering
gibberings, and Babion babbling-like, to hoot
out of countenance all modest measure, as if our
sins were not sufficing to stoop our backs without He wresting and crooking his members to
mistimed mirth (rather malice) in deformed
fashion, leering when he should learn, prating
for praying, goggling his eyes (better upturned
for grace), whereas in Paradice (if we can go
thus high for His professions) that devilish Serpent appeareth his undoubted Predecessor, first
induing a mask like some roguish roistering
Roscius (I spit at them all) to beguile with
stage shows the gaping Woman, whose Sex
hath still chiefly upheld these Mysteries, and
are voiced to be the chief Stage-haunters, where,
as I am told, the custom is commonly to mumble
(between acts) apples, not ambiguously derived
from that pernicious Pippin (worse in effect than
the Apples of Discord), whereas sometimes the
hissing sounds of displeasure, as I hear, do
lively reintonate that snake-taking-leave, and
diabolical goings off, in Paradice.'

The Puritanic effervescence of the early
Presbyterians appears to have abated with time,

and the opinions of the more immediate ancestors of our subject to have subsided at length
into a strain of moderate Calvinism. Still, a
tincture of the old leaven was to be expected
among the posterity of A. L.

Our hero was an only son of Habakkuk
Liston, settled as an Anabaptist minister upon
the patrimonial soil of his ancestors. A regular
certificate appears, thus entered in the Church-
book at Lupton Magna : ' *Johannes, filius
Habakkuk et Rebeccæ Liston, Dissentientium,
natus quinto Decembri,* 1780, *baptizatus sexto
Februarii sequentis ; Sponsoribus J. et W. Wool-
laston, una cum Maria Merryweather.*' The
singularity of an Anabaptist minister conforming
to the child-rites of the Church would have
tempted me to doubt the authenticity of this
entry, had I not been obliged with the actual
sight of it by the favour of Mr. Minns, the intelligent and worthy parish clerk of Lupton.
Possibly some expectation in point of worldly
advantages from some of the sponsors might have
induced this unseemly deviation, as it must have
appeared, from the practice and principles of that
generally rigid sect. The term *Dissentientium*
was possibly intended by the orthodox clergyman as a slur upon the supposed inconsistency.
What, or of what nature, the expectations we

have hinted at may have been, we have now no means of ascertaining. Of the Woollastons no trace is now discoverable in the village. The name of Merryweather occurs over the front of a grocer's shop at the western extremity of Lupton.

Of the infant Liston we find no events recorded before his fourth year, in which a severe attack of the measels bid fair to have robbed the rising generation of a fund of innocent entertainment. He had it of the confluent kind, as it is called ; and the child's life was for a week or two despaired of. His recovery he always attributes (under Heaven) to the humane interference of one Dr. Wilhelm Richter, a German empiric, who in this extremity prescribed a copious diet of *sauer-kraut,* which the child was observed to reach at with avidity, when other food repelled him ; and from this change of diet his restoration was rapid and complete. We have often heard him name the circumstance with gratitude ; and it is not altogether surprising that a relish for this kind of aliment, so abhorrent and harsh to common English palates, has accompanied him through life. When any of Mr. Liston's intimates invite him to supper, he never fails of finding, nearest to his knife and fork, a dish of *sauer-kraut.*

At the age of nine we find our subject under the tuition of the Rev. Mr. Goodenough (his father's health not permitting him, probably, to instruct him himself), by whom he was inducted into a competent portion of Latin and Greek, with some mathematics, till the death of Mr. Goodenough, in his own seventieth and Master Liston's eleventh year, put a stop for the present to his classical progress.

We have heard our hero, with emotions which do his heart honour, describe the awful circumstances attending the decease of this worthy old gentleman. It seems they had been walking out together, master and pupil, in a fine sunset to the distance of three-quarters of a mile west of Lupton, when a sudden curiosity took Mr. Goodenough to look down upon a chasm where a shaft had been lately sunk in a mining speculation (then projecting, but abandoned soon after, as not answering the promised success, by Sir Ralph Shepperton, knight and member for the county). The old clergyman, leaning over, either with incaution or sudden giddiness (probably a mixture of both), suddenly lost his footing, and, to use Mr. Liston's phrase, disappeared, and was doubtless broken into a thousand pieces. The sound of his head, etc., dashing successively upon the projecting masses of the chasm, had such an effect upon the child that a serious sickness ensued; and even for many years after his recovery, he was not once seen so much as to smile.

The joint death of both his parents, which happened not many months after this disastrous accident, and were probably (one or both of them) accelerated by it, threw our youth upon the protection of his maternal great-aunt, Mrs. Sittingbourn. Of this aunt we have never heard him speak but with expressions amounting almost to reverence. To the influence of her early counsels and manners he has always attributed the firmness with which, in maturer years, thrown upon a way of life commonly not the best adapted to gravity and self-retirement, he has been able to maintain a serious character, untinctured with the levities incident to his profession. Ann Sittingbourn (we have seen her portrait by Hudson) was stately, stiff, tall, with a cast of features strikingly resembling the subject of this memoir. Her estate in Kent was spacious and well-wooded; the house one of those venerable old mansions which are so impressive in childhood, and so hardly forgotten in succeeding years. In the venerable solitudes of Charnwood, among thick shades of the oak and beech (this last his favourite tree) the young

Liston cultivated those contemplative habits which have never entirely deserted him in after years. Here he was commonly in the summer months to be met with, with a book in his hand, — not a play-book, — meditating. Boyle's ' Reflections ' was at one time the darling volume ; which, in its turn, was superseded by Young's ' Night Thoughts,' which has continued its hold upon him through life. He carries it always about him ; and it is no uncommon thing for him to be seen, in the refreshing intervals of his occupation, leaning against a side-scene, in a sort of Herbert-of-Cherbury posture, turning over a pocket-edition of his favourite author.

But the solitudes of Charnwood were not destined always to obscure the path of our young hero. The premature death of Mrs. Sittingbourn, at the age of seventy, occasioned by incautious burning of a pot of charcoal in her sleeping-chamber, left him in his nineteenth year nearly without resources. That the stage at all should have presented itself as an eligible scope for his talents, and, in particular, that he should have chosen a line so foreign to what appears to have been his turn of mind, may require some explanation.

At Charnwood, then, we behold him, thoughtful, grave, ascetic. From his cradle averse to flesh-meats and strong drink; abstemious even beyond the genius of the place, and almost in spite of the remonstrances of his great-aunt, who, though strict, was not rigid, — water was his habitual drink, and his food little beyond the mast and beech-nuts of his favourite groves. It is a medical fact that this kind of diet, however favourable to the contemplative powers of the primitive hermits, etc., is but ill-adapted to the less robust minds and bodies of a later generation. Hypochondria almost constantly ensues. It was so in the case of the young Liston. He was subject to sights, and had visions. Those arid beech-nuts, distilled by a complexion naturally adust, mounted into an occiput already prepared to kindle by long seclusion and the fervour of strict Calvinistic notions. In the glooms of Charnwood he was assailed by illusions similar in kind to those which are related of the famous Anthony of Padua. Wild antic faces would ever and anon protrude themselves upon his sensorium. Whether he shut his eyes, or kept them open, the same illusions operated. The darker and more profound were his cogitations, the droller and more whimsical became the apparitions. They buzzed about him thick as flies, flapping at him, flouting him, hooting in his ear, yet with such comic appendages that what at first was his bane became at length his solace ; and he desired no better society than that of his merry phantasmata. We shall presently find in what way this remarkable phenomenon influenced his future destiny.

On the death of Mrs. Sittingbourn we find him received into the family of Mr. Willoughby, an eminent Turkey merchant, resident in Birchin Lane, London. We lose a little whilê here the chain of his history, — by what inducements this gentleman was determined to make him an inmate of his house. Probably he had had some personal kindness for Mrs. Sittingbourn formerly ; but however it was, the young man was here treated more like a son than a clerk, though he was nominally but the latter. Different avocations, the change of scene, with that alternation of business and recreation which in its greatest perfection is to be had only in London, appear to have weaned him in a short time from the hypochondriacal affections which had beset him at Charnwood.

In the three years which followed his removal to Birchin Lane, we find him making more than one voyage to the Levant, as chief factor for

Mr. Willoughby at the Porte. We could easily fill our biography with the pleasant passages which we have heard him relate as having happened to him at Constantinople, — such as his having been taken up on suspicion of a design of penetrating the seraglio, etc. ; but, with the deepest convincement of this gentleman's own veracity, we think that some of the stories are of that whimsical, and others of that romantic nature, which, however diverting, would be out of place in a narrative of this kind, which aims not only at strict truth, but at avoiding the very appearance of the contrary.

We will now bring him over the seas again, and suppose him in the counting-house in Birchin Lane, his protector satisfied with the returns of his factorage, and all going on so smoothly that we may expect to find Mr. Liston at last an opulent merchant upon 'Change, as it is called. But see the turns of destiny! Upon a summer's excursion into Norfolk, in the year 1801, the accidental sight of pretty Sally Parker, as she was called (then in the Norwich company), diverted his inclinations at once from commerce, and he became, in the language of commonplace biography, stage-struck. Happy for the lovers of mirth was it that our hero took this turn ; he might

else have been to this hour that unentertain-
ing character, a plodding London merchant.

We accordingly find him shortly after making
his *début*, as it is called, upon the Norwich
boards, in the season of that year, being then
in the twenty-second year of his age. Having
a natural bent to tragedy, he chose the part of
Pyrrhus, in the ' Distressed Mother,' to Sally
Parker's Hermione. We find him afterwards
as Barnwell, Altamont, Chamont, etc. ; but as
if Nature had destined him to the sock, an un-
avoidable infirmity absolutely discapacitated him
for tragedy. His person, at this latter period
of which I have been speaking, was graceful,
and even commanding ; his countenance set to
gravity: he had the power of arresting the attention of an audience at first sight almost beyond
any other tragic actor. But he could not hold
it. To understand this obstacle, we must go
back a few years to those appalling reveries at
Charnwood. Those illusions, which had van-
ished before the dissipation of a less recluse
life and more free society, now in his solitary
tragic studies, and amid the intense calls upon
feeling incident to tragic acting, came back
upon him with tenfold vividness. In the midst
of some most pathetic passage (the parting of
Jaffier with his dying friend, for instance), he

G

would suddenly be surprised with a fit of violent horse-laughter. While the spectators were all sobbing before him with emotion, suddenly one of those grotesque faces would peep out upon him, and he could not resist the impulse. A timely excuse once or twice served his purpose, but no audiences could be expected to bear repeatedly this violation of the continuity of feeling. He describes them (the illusions) as so many demons haunting him, and paralyzing every effect. Even now, I am told, he cannot recite the famous soliloquy in ' Hamlet,' even in private, without immoderate bursts of laughter. However, what he had not force of reason sufficient to overcome, he had good sense enough to turn into emolument, and determined to make a commodity of his distemper. He prudently exchanged the buskin for the sock, and the illusions instantly ceased; or, if they occurred for a short season, by their very co-operation added a zest to his comic vein, — some of his most catching faces being (as he expresses it) little more than transcripts and copies of those extraordinary phantasmata.

We have now drawn out our hero's existence to the period when he was about to meet, for the first time, the sympathies of a London audience. The particulars of his success since have been too much before our eyes to render a circumstantial detail of them expedient. I shall only mention that Mr. Willoughby, his resentments having had time to subside, is at present one of the fastest friends of his old renegade factor ; and that, Mr. Liston's hopes of Miss Parker vanishing along with his unsuccessful suit to Melpomene, in the autumn of 1811 he married his present lady, by whom he has been blessed with one son, Philip, and two daughters, Ann and Augustina.

TO THE SHADE OF ELLISTON.

JOYOUSEST of once embodied spirits, whither at length hast thou flown ? to what genial region are we permitted to conjecture that thou hast flitted ?

Art thou sowing thy WILD OATS yet (the harvest time was still to come with thee) upon casual sands of Avernus ? or art thou enacting ROVER (as we would gladlier think) by wandering Elysian streams ?

This mortal frame, while thou didst play thy brief antics amongst us, was in truth anything but a prison to thee, as the vain Platonist dreams of this *body* to be no better than a county gaol, forsooth, or some house of durance vile, whereof the five senses are the fetters. Thou knewest better than to be in a hurry to cast off these gyves ; and had notice to quit, I fear, before thou wert quite ready to abandon this fleshy tenement. It was thy Pleasure-House, thy Palace of Dainty Devices ; thy Louvre, or thy Whitehall.

What new mysterious lodgings dost thou tenant now ? or when may we expect thy aërial house-warming ?

Tartarus we know, and we have read of the Blessed Shades ; now cannot I intelligibly fancy thee in either.

Is it too much to hazard a conjecture that (as the Schoolmen admitted a receptacle apart for patriarchs and unchrisom babes) there may exist — not far perchance from that store-house of all vanities which Milton saw in visions — a LIMBO somewhere for PLAYERS ? and that

> Up thither like aërial vapours fly
> Both all Stage things, and all that in Stage things
> Built their fond hopes of glory, or lasting fame ?
> All the unaccomplished works of Authors' hands,
> Abortive, monstrous, or unkindly mixed,
> Damn'd upon earth, fleet thither, —
> Play, Opera, Farce, with all their trumpery.

There, by the neighbouring moon (by some not improperly supposed thy Regent Planet upon earth), mayst thou not still be acting thy managerial pranks, great disembodied Lessee ? but Lessee still, and still a manager ?

In Green Rooms, impervious to mortal eye, the muse beholds thee wielding posthumous empire.

Thin ghosts of Figurantes (never plump on earth) circle thee in endlessly, and still their song is, *Fie on sinful Phantasy !*

Magnificent were thy capriccios on this globe of earth, ROBERT WILLIAM ELLISTON ! for as yet we know not thy new name in heaven.

It irks me to think that, stripped of thy regalities, thou shouldst ferry over, a poor forked shade, in crazy Stygian wherry. Methinks I hear the old boatman, paddling by the weedy wharf, with raucid voice bawling 'SCULLS, SCULLS !' to which, with waving hand and majestic action, thou deignest no reply other than in two curt monosyllables, ' No : Oars.'

But the laws of Pluto's kingdom know small difference between king and cobbler, manager and call-boy ; and if haply your dates of life were conterminant, you are quietly taking your passage, cheek by cheek (oh, ignoble levelling of Death !) with the shade of some recently departed candle-snuffer.

But mercy ! what strippings, what tearing off of histrionic robes, and private vanities ! what denudations to the bone, before the surly Ferryman will admit you to set a foot within his battered lighter !

Crowns, sceptres ; shield, sword, and truncheon ; thy own coronation robes (for thou hast brought the whole property-man's wardrobe with thee, enough to sink a navy) ; the judge's ermine, the coxcomb's wig, the snuff-box *à la Foppington*, — all must overboard, he positively swears. And that Ancient Mariner brooks no denial ; for since the tiresome monodrame of the old Thracian Harper, Charon, it is to be believed, hath shown small taste for theatricals.

Ay, now 't is done. You are just boat-weight ; *pura et puta anima.*

But, bless me, how *little* you look !

So shall we all look, kings and kaisers, — stripped for the last voyage.

But the murky rogue pushes off. Adieu, pleasant and thrice-pleasant shade ! with my parting thanks for many a heavy hour of life lightened by thy harmless extravaganzas, public or domestic.

Rhadamanthus, — who tries the lighter causes below, leaving to his two brethren the heavy calendars, — honest Rhadamanth, always partial to players, weighing their party-coloured existence here upon earth, making account of the few foibles that may have shaded thy *real life*, as we call it (though, substantially, scarcely less a vapour than thy idlest vagaries upon the boards of the Drury), as but of so many echoes, natural re-percussions, and results to be expected from the assumed extravagancies of thy *secondary*, or *mock life*, nightly upon a stage, — after a lenient castigation with rods lighter than of those Medusean ringlets, but just enough to 'whip the offending Adam out of thee,' shall courteously dismiss thee at the right-hand gate — the O. P. side of Hades — that conducts to masques and merry-makings in the Theatre Royal of Proserpine.

PLAUDITO ET VALETO.

ELLISTONIANA.

MY acquaintance with the pleasant creature, whose loss we all deplore, was but slight. My first introduction to E., which afterwards ripened into an acquaintance a little on this side of intimacy, was over a counter in the Leamington Spa Library, then newly entered upon by a branch of his family. E., whom nothing misbecame, — to auspicate, I suppose, the filial concern, and set it a-going with a lustre, — was serving in person two damsels fair who had come into the shop ostensibly to inquire for some new publication, but in reality to have a sight of the illustrious shopman, hoping some conference. With what an air did he reach down the volume, dispassionately giving his opinion of the worth of the work in question, and launching out into a dissertation on its comparative merits with those of certain publications of a similar stamp, its rivals! his enchanted customers fairly hanging on his lips, subdued to their authoritative sentence. So have I seen a gentleman in comedy *acting* the shopman. So Lovelace sold his gloves in King Street. I admired the histrionic art by which he contrived to carry clean away every notion of disgrace from the occupation he had so generously submitted to ; and from that hour I judged him, with no after repentance, to be a person with whom it would be a felicity to be more acquainted.

To descant upon his merits as a comedian would be superfluous. With his blended private and professional habits alone I have to do,—that harmonious fusion of the manners of the player into those of every-day life which brought the stage-boards into streets and dining-parlours, and kept up the play when the play was ended. ' I like Wrench,' a friend was saying to him, one day, ' because he is the same natural, easy creature *on* the stage that he is *off*.' ' My case exactly,' retorted Elliston, with a charming forgetfulness that the converse of a proposition does not always lead to the same conclusion ; ' I am the same person *off* the stage that I am *on*.' The inference at first sight seems identical ; but examine it a little, and it confesses only that the one performer was never, and the other always, *acting*.

And in truth this was the charm of Elliston's

private deportment. You had spirited performance always going on before your eyes, with
nothing to pay. As where a monarch takes up
his casual abode for the night, the poorest hovel
which he honours by his sleeping in it becomes
ipso facto for that time a palace, so wherever
Elliston walked, sat, or stood still, there was
the theatre. He carried about with him his pit,
boxes, and galleries, and set up his portable
play-house at corners of streets and in the
market-places. Upon flintiest pavements he
trod the boards still ; and if his theme chanced
to be passionate, the green baize carpet of
tragedy spontaneously rose beneath his feet.
Now, this was hearty, and showed a love for his
art. So Apelles *always* painted, — in thought.
So G. D. *always* poetizes. I hate a lukewarm
artist. I have known actors — and some of
them of Elliston's own stamp — who shall have
agreeably been amusing you in the part of a
rake or a coxcomb, through the two or three
hours of their dramatic existence ; but no sooner
does the curtain fall with its leaden clatter, but
a spirit of lead seems to seize on all their faculties. They emerge sour, morose persons, in-
tolerable to their families, servants, etc. Another
shall have been expanding your heart with generous deeds and sentiments till it even beats with

yearnings of universal sympathy ; you absolutely long to go home and do some good action. The play seems tedious till you can get fairly out of the house and realize your laudable intentions.   At length the final bell rings, and this cordial representative of all that is amiable in human breasts steps forth, — a miser.   Elliston was more of a piece.   Did he *play* Ranger, and did Ranger fill the general bosom of the town with satisfaction ?   Why should *he* not be Ranger, and diffuse the same cordial satisfaction among his private circles ?   With *his* temperament, *his* animal spirits, *his* good-nature, his follies, perchance, could he do better than identify himself with his impersonation ?   Are we to like a pleasant rake, or coxcomb, on the stage, and give ourselves airs of aversion for the identical character presented to us in actual life ?   or what would the performer have gained by divesting himself of the impersonation ?   Could the man Elliston have been essentially different from his part, even if he had avoided to reflect to us studiously, in private circles, the airy briskness, the forwardness, the 'scape-goat trickeries of the prototype ?

    ' But there is something not natural in this everlasting *acting ;* we want the real man.'

    Are you quite sure that it is not the man him-

self, whom you cannot, or will not, see under
some adventitious trappings, which, nevertheless,
sit not at all inconsistently upon him ? What if it
is the nature of some men to be highly artificial ?
The fault is least reprehensible in *players.*
Cibber was his own Foppington, with almost
as much wit as Vanbrugh could add to it.

'My conceit of his person' — it is Ben
Jonson speaking of Lord Bacon — 'was never
increased towards him by his *place* or *honours.*
But I have and do reverence him for the
greatness that was only proper to himself ; in
that he seemed to me ever one of the *greatest*
men that had been in many ages. In his adver-
sity I ever prayed that Heaven would give him
strength ; for *greatness* he could not want.'

The quality here commended was scarcely
less conspicuous in the subject of these idle
reminiscences than in my Lord Verulam. Those
who have imagined that an unexpected elevation
to the direction of a great London theatre affected the consequence of Elliston, or at all
changed his nature, knew not the essential
greatness of the man whom they disparage. It
was my fortune to encounter him near St.
Dunstan's Church (which, with its punctual
giants, is now no more than dust and a shadow),
on the morning of his election to that high

office. Grasping my hand with a look of sig-
nificance, he only uttered, ' Have you heard
the news ? ' Then, with another look following
up the blow, he subjoined, ' I am the future manager of Drury Lane Theatre.' Breathless as
he saw me, he stayed not for congratulation or
reply, but mutely stalked away, leaving me to
chew upon his new-blown dignities at leisure.
In fact, nothing could be said to it. Expressive
silence alone could muse his praise. This was
in his *great* style.

But was he less *great* (be witness, O ye powers
of Equanimity that supported in the ruins of
Carthage the consular exile, and more recently
transmuted, for a more illustrious exile, the
barren constableship of Elba into an image of
Imperial France) when, in melancholy after-
years, again, much near the same spot, I met
him, when that sceptre had been wrested from
his hand, and his dominion was curtailed to the
petty managership and part proprietorship of
the small Olympic, *his Elba?* He still played
nightly upon the boards of Drury, but in parts,
alas! allotted to him, not magnificently dis-
tributed by him. Waiving his great loss as
nothing, and magnificently sinking the sense
of fallen *material* grandeur in the more liberal
resentment of depreciations done to his more

lofty *intellectual* pretensions, ' Have you heard' (his customary exordium) — ' have you heard,' said he, ' how they treat me ? They put me in *comedy*.' Thought I, — but his finger on his lips forbade any verbal interruption, — ' Where could they have put you better ?' Then, after a pause, — ' Where I formerly played Romeo, I now play Mercutio ; ' and so again he stalked away, neither staying nor caring for responses.

Oh ! it was a rich scene — but Sir A—— C——, the best of story-tellers and surgeons, who mends a lame narrative almost as well as he sets a fracture, alone could do justice to it — that I was a witness to in the tarnished room (that had once been green) of that same little Olympic. There, after his deposition from Imperial Drury, he substituted a throne. That Olympic Hill was his ' highest heaven ; ' himself ' Jove in his chair.' There he sat in state, while before him, on complaint of prompter, was brought for judgment — how shall I describe her ? — one of those little tawdry things that flirt at the tails of choruses, a probationer for the town in either of its senses, the pertest little drab, a dirty fringe and appendage of the lamp's smoke, who, it seems, on some disapprobation expressed by a ' highly respectable ' audience had precipitately quitted her station on the boards, and withdrawn her small talents in disgust.

' And how dare you,' said her manager, assuming a censorial severity which would have crushed the confidence of a Vestris, and disarmed that beautiful Rebel herself of her professional caprices, — I verily believe he thought *her* standing before him, — ' how dare you, madam, withdraw yourself, without a notice, from your theatrical duties ? ' ' I was hissed, sir.' ' And you have the presumption to decide upon the taste of the town ? ' ' I don't know that, sir, but I will never stand to be hissed,' was the subjoinder of young Confidence. When, gathering up his features into one significant mass of wonder, pity, and expostulatory indignation, in a lesson never to have been lost upon a creature less forward than she who stood before him, his words were these : ' They have hissed *me*.'

'T was the identical argument à *fortiori* which the son of Peleus uses to Lycaon trembling under his lance, to persuade him to take his destiny with a good grace. ' I too am mortal.' And it is to be believed that in both cases the rhetoric missed of its application for want of a proper understanding with the faculties of the respective recipients.

' Quite an Opera pit,' he said to me as he was courteously conducting me over the benches of his Surrey Theatre, — the last retreat and recess of his every-day waning grandeur.

Those who knew Elliston, will know the *manner* in which he pronounced the latter sentence of the few words I am about to record. One proud day to me he took his roast mutton with us in the Temple, to which I had superadded a preliminary haddock. After a rather plentiful partaking of the meagre banquet, not unrefreshed with the humbler sort of liquors, I made a sort of apology for the humility of the fare, observing that for my own part I never ate but of one dish at dinner. ' I too never eat but one thing at dinner,' was his reply ; then, after a pause, — ' reckoning fish as nothing.' The manner was all. It was as if by one peremptory sentence he had decreed the annihilation of all the savoury esculents which the pleasant and nutritious-food-giving Ocean pours forth upon poor humans from her watery bosom. This was *greatness,* tempered with considerate *tenderness* to the feelings of his scanty but welcoming entertainer.

Great wert thou in thy life, Robert William Elliston ! and *not lessened* in thy death, if report speak truly, which says that thou didst direct

H

that thy mortal remains should repose under no inscription but one of pure *Latinity*. Classical was thy bringing up! and beautiful was the feeling on thy last bed, which, connecting the man with the boy, took thee back to thy latest exercise of imagination, to the days when, undreaming of Theatres and Managerships, thou wert a scholar, and an early ripe one, under the roofs builded by the munificent and pious Colet. For thee the Pauline Muses weep. In elegies, that shall silence this crude prose, they shall celebrate thy praise.

THE RELIGION OF ACTORS.

THE world has hitherto so little troubled its head upon the points of doctrine held by a community which contributes in other ways so largely to its amusement, that, before the late mischance of a celebrated tragic actor, it scarce condescended to look into the practice of any individual player, much less to inquire into the hidden and abscondite springs of his actions. Indeed, it is with some violence to the imagination that we conceive of an actor as belonging to the relations of private life, so closely do we identify these persons in our mind with the characters which they assume upon the stage. How oddly does it sound when we are told that the late Miss Pope, for instance, — that is to say, in our notion of her Mrs. Candour, — was a good daughter, an affectionate sister, and exemplary in all the parts of domestic life! With still greater difficulty can we carry our notions to church, and conceive of Liston kneeling upon a hassock, or

Munden uttering a pious ejaculation,—" making mouths at the invisible event." But the times are fast improving; and if the process of sanctity begun under the happy auspices of the present licenser go on to its completion, it will be as necessary for a comedian to give an account of his faith as of his conduct. Fawcett must study the five points, and Dicky Suett, if he were alive, would have to rub up his catechism. Already the effects of it begin to appear. A celebrated performer has thought fit to oblige the world with a confession of his faith, or Br——'s *Religio Dramatici.* This gentleman, in his laudable attempt to shift from his person the obloquy of Judaism, with a forwardness of a new convert in trying to prove too much, has, in the opinion of many, proved too little. A simple declaration of his Christianity was sufficient; but, strange to say, his apology has not a word about it. We are left to gather it from some expressions which imply that he is a Protestant; but we did not wish to inquire into the niceties of his orthodoxy. To his friends of the *old persuasion* the distinction was impertinent; for what cares Rabbi Ben Kimchi for the differences which have split our novelty? To the great body of Christians that holds the Pope's supremacy

— that is to say, to the major part of the Christian world — his religion will appear as much to seek as ever. But perhaps he conceived that all Christians are Protestants, as children and the common people call all, that are not animals, Christians. The mistake was not very considerable in so young a proselyte, or he might think the general (as logicians speak) involved in the particular. All Protestants are Christians; but I am a Protestant; *ergo*, etc. : as if a marmoset, contending to be a man, overleaping that term as too generic and vulgar, should at once roundly proclaim himself to be a gentleman. The argument would be, as we say, *exabundanti.* From whichever course this *excessus in terminis* proceeded, we can do no less than congratulate the general state of Christendom upon the accession of so extraordinary a convert. Who was the happy instrument of the conversion, we are yet to learn: it comes nearest to the attempt of the late pious Dr. Watts to Christianize the Psalms of the Old Testament. Something of the old Hebrew racinesss is lost in the transfusion, but much of its asperity is softened and pared down in the adaptation.

The appearance of so singular a treatise at this conjuncture has set us upon an inquiry into the present state of religion upon the stage generally. By the favour of the Churchwardens of St. Martin's-in-the-Fields, and St. Paul's, Covent Garden, who have very readily, and with great kindness, assisted our pursuit, we are enabled to lay before the public the following particulars. Strictly speaking, neither of the two great bodies is collectively a religious institution. We expected to find a chaplain among them, as at St Stephen's and other court establishments ; and were the more surprised at the omission, as the last Mr. Bengough at the one house, and Mr. Powell at the other, from a gravity of speech and demeanour, and the habit of wearing black at their first appearances in the beginning of the *fifth* or the conclusion of the *fourth* act, so eminently pointed out their qualifications for such office. These corporations, then, being not properly congregational, we must seek the solution of our question in the tastes, attainments, accidental breeding, and education of the individual members of them. As we were prepared to expect, a majority at both houses adhere to the religion of the Church Established, — only that at one of them a strong leaven of Roman Catholicism is suspected ; which, considering the notorious education of the manager at a

foreign seminary, is not so much to be wondered
at. Some have gone so far as to report that
Mr. T——y, in particular, belongs to an order
lately restored on the Continent. We can con-
tradict this ; that gentleman is a member of the
Kirk of Scotland, and his name is to be found,
much to his honour, in the list of seceders from
the congregation of Mr. Fletcher. While the
generality, as we have said, are content to jog
on in the safe trammels of national orthodoxy,
symptoms of a sectarian spirit have broken out
in quarters where we should least have looked
for it. Some of the ladies at both houses are
deep in controverted points. Miss F——e,
we are credibly informed, is a *Sub-* and Madame
V—— a *Supra-*Lapsarian. Mr. Pope is the
last of the exploded sect of the Ranters. Mr.
Sinclair has joined the Shakers. Mr. Grimaldi,
Sen., after being long a Jumper, has lately
fallen into some whimsical theories respecting
the fall of man, which he understands, not of
an allegorical, but a *real tumble,* — by which the
whole body of humanity became, as it were,
lame to the performance of good works. Pride
he will have to be nothing but a stiff neck ;
irresolution, the nerves shaken ; an inclination
to sinister paths, crookedness of the joints ;
spiritual deadness, a paralysis ; want of charity,

a contraction in the fingers ; despising of government, a broken head ; the plaster, a sermon ; the lint to bind it up, the text ; the probers, the preachers ; a pair of crutches, the old and new law ; a bandage, religious obligation, —a fanciful mode of illustration, derived from the accidents and habits of his past calling *spiritualized*, rather than from any accurate acquaintance with the Hebrew text, in which report speaks him but a raw scholar. Mr. Elliston, from all we can learn, has his religion yet to choose ; though some think him a Muggletonian.

ON THE CUSTOM OF HISSING AT THE THEATRES.

WITH SOME ACCOUNT OF A CLUB OF DAMNED AUTHORS.

M R. REFLECTOR, — I am one of those persons whom the world has thought proper to designate by the title of Damned Authors. In that memorable season of dramatic failures, 1806–7, — in which no fewer, I think, than two tragedies, four comedies, one opera, and three farces suffered at Drury Lane Theatre, — I was found guilty of constructing an afterpiece, and was *damned.*

Against the decision of the public in such instances there can be no appeal. The Clerk of Chatham might as well have protested against the decision.of Cade and his followers, who were then *the public.* Like him, I was condemned because I could write.

Not but it did appear to some of us that the measures of the popular tribunal at that period savoured a little of harshness and of the *summum*

jus. The public mouth was early in the season
fleshed upon the ' Vindictive Man ' and some
pieces of that nature ; and it retained through
the remainder of it a relish of blood.   As Dr.
Johnson would have said, ' Sir, there was a
habit of sibilation in the house.'

Still less am I disposed to inquire into the
reason of the comparative lenity, on the other
hand, with which some pieces were treated,
which, to indifferent judges, seemed at least as
much deserving of condemnation as some of
those which met with it.   I am willing to put
a favourable construction upon the votes that
were given against us ; I believe that there was
no bribery or designed partiality in the case :
only ' our nonsense did not happen to suit their
nonsense ; ' that was all.

But against the *manner* in which the public,
on these occasions, think fit to deliver their disapprobation, I must and ever will protest.

Sir, imagine — but you have been present at
the damning of a piece ; those who never had
that felicity, I beg them to imagine — a vast
theatre, like that which Drury Lane was before
it was a heap of dust and ashes (I insult not over
its fallen greatness ; let it recover itself when it
can, for me, let it lift up its towering head once
more, and take in poor authors to write for it, —

hic cæstus artemque repono), — a theatre like that, filled with all sorts of disgusting sounds, — shrieks, groans, hisses, but chiefly the last, like the noise of many waters, or that which Don Quixote heard from the fulling-mills, or that wilder combination of devilish sounds which Saint Anthony listened to in the wilderness.

Oh! Mr. Reflector, is it not a pity that the sweet human voice, which was given man to speak with, to sing with, to whisper tones of love in, to express compliance, to convey a favour, or to grant a suit, — that voice which in a Siddons or a Braham rouses us, in a Siren Catalani charms and captivates us, — that the musical, expressive human voice should be converted into a rival of the noises of silly geese and irrational, venomous snakes?

I never shall forget the sounds on *my night.* I never before that time fully felt the reception which the Author of All Ill, in the ' Paradise Lost ' meeets with from the critics in the *pit,* at the final close of his Tragedy upon the Human Race, — though that, alas! met with too much success : —

> From innumerable tongues
> A dismal universal *hiss,* — the sound
> Of public scorn.   Dreadful was the din
> Of *hissing* through the hall, thick swarming now

With complicated monsters, head and tail,
Scorpion and asp, and Amphisbæna dire,
Cerastes horn'd, Hydrus, and Elops drear,
And Dipsas.

For *hall* substitute *theatre*, and you have the very image of what takes place at what is called the *damnation* of a piece, — and properly so called ; for here you see its origin plainly, whence the custom was derived, and what the first piece was that so suffered.   After this, none can doubt the propriety of the appellation.

But, sir, as to the justice of bestowing such appalling, heart-withering denunciations of the popular obloquy upon the venial mistake of a poor author, who thought to please us in the act of filling his pockets, — for the sum of his demerits amounts to no more than that, — it does, I own, seem to me a species of retributive justice far too severe for the offence.   A culprit in the pillory (bate the eggs) meets with no severer exprobration.

Indeed, I have often wondered that some modest critic has not proposed that there should be a wooden machine to that effect erected in some convenient part of the proscenium, which an unsuccessful author should be required to mount and stand his hour, exposed to the apples and oranges of the pit.   This *amende hono-*

rable would well suit with the meanness of some authors, who in their prologues fairly prostrate their skulls to the audience, and seem to invite a pelting.

Or why should they not have their pens publicly broke over their heads, as the swords of recreant knights in old times were, and an oath administered to them that they should never write again?

Seriously, *Messieurs the Public*, this outrageous way which you have got of expressing your displeasures is too much for the occasion. When I was deafening under the effects of it, I could not help asking what crime of great moral turpitude I had committed; for every man about me seemed to feel the offence as personal to himself, as something which public interest and private feelings alike called upon him in the strongest possible manner to stigmatize with infamy.

The Romans, it is well known to you, Mr. Reflector, took a gentler method of marking their disapprobation of an author's work. They were a humane and equitable nation. They left the *furca* and the *patibulum*, the axe and the rods, to great offenders; for these minor and (if I may so term them) extra-moral offences, *the bent-thumb* was considered as a sufficient sign of disapprobation, — *vertere pollicem;* as *the pressed thumb, premere pollicem,* was a mark of approving.

And really there seems to have been a sort of fitness in this method, a correspondency of sign in the punishment to the offence. For as the action of *writing* is performed by bending the thumb forward, the retroversion, or bending back, of that joint did not unaptly point to the *opposite of that action;* implying that it was the will of the audience that the author should *write no more,* — a much more significant as well as more humane way of expressing that desire than our custom of hissing, which is altogether sense- less and indefensible. Nor do we find that the Roman audiences deprived themselves, by this lenity, of any tittle of that supremacy which au- diences in all ages have thought themselves bound to maintain over such as have been can- didates for their applause. On the contrary, by this method they seem to have had the author, as we should express it, completely *under finger and thumb.*

The provocations to which a dramatic genius is exposed from the public are so much the more vexatious as they are removed from any possibility of retaliation, which sweetens most other injuries; for the public *never writes it-*

self. Not but something very like it took place at the time of the O. P. differences. The placards which were nightly exhibited were, properly speaking, the composition of the public. The public wrote them, the public applauded them ; and precious *morceaux* of wit and eloquence they were, — except some few of a better quality, which it is well known were furnished by professed dramatic writers. After this specimen of what the public can do for itself, it should be a little slow in condemning what others do for it.

As the degrees of malignancy vary in people according as they have more or less of the Old Serpent (the father of hisses) in their composition, I have sometimes amused myself with analyzing this many-headed hydra, which calls itself the public, into the component parts of which it is ' complicated, head and tail,' and seeing how many varieties of the snake kind it can afford.

First, there is the Common English Snake. — This is that part of the auditory who are always the majority at damnations, but who, having no critical venom in themselves to sting them on, stay till they hear others hiss, and then join ın for company.

The Blind Worm is a species very nearly

allied to the foregoing.   Some naturalists have doubted whether they are not the same.

The Rattlesnake. — These are your obstreperous talking critics, — the impertinent guides of the pit, — who will not give a plain man leave to enjoy an evening's entertainment, but with their frothy jargon and incessant finding of faults, either drown his pleasure quite, or force him, in his own defence, to join in their clamorous censure.   The hiss always originates with these. When this creature springs his *rattle*, you would think, from the noise it makes, there was something in it ; but you have only to examine the instrument from which the noise proceeds, and you will find it typical of a critic's tongue, — a shallow membrane, empty, voluble, and seated in the most contemptible part of the creature's body.

The Whipsnake. — This is he that lashes the poor author the next day in the newspapers.

The Deaf Adder, or *Surda Echidna* of Linnæus. — Under this head may be classed all that portion of the spectators (for audience they properly are not) who, not finding the first act of a piece answer to their preconceived notions of what a first act should be, like Obstinate in John Bunyan, positively thrust their fingers in their ears, that they may not hear a word of what is coming, though perhaps the very next act may be composed in a style as different as possible, and be written quite to their own tastes. These adders refuse to hear the voice of the charmer, because the tuning of his instrument gave him offence.

I should weary you and myself too if I were to go through all the classes of the serpent kind. Two qualities are common to them all, — they are creatures of remarkably cold digestions, and chiefly haunt *pits* and low grounds.

I proceed with more pleasure to give you an account of a club to which I have the honour to belong. There are fourteen of us, who are all authors that have been once in our lives what is called ' damned.' We meet on the anniversary of our respective nights, and make ourselves merry at the expense of the public. The chief tenets which distinguish our society, and which every man among us is bound to hold for gospel, are —

That the public, or mob, in all ages have been a set of blind, deaf, obstinate, senseless, illiterate savages. That no man of genius, in his senses, would be ambitious of pleasing such a capricious, ungrateful rabble. That the only legitimate end of writing for them is to pick their pockets ;

I

and, that failing, we are at full liberty to vilify and abuse them as much as ever we think fit.

That authors, by their affected pretences to humility, which they made use of as a cloak to insinuate their writings into the callous senses of the multitude, obtuse to everything but the grossest flattery, have by degrees made that great beast their master, — as we may act submission to children till we are obliged to practise it in earnest. That authors are and ought to be considered the masters and preceptors of the public, and not *vice versâ*. That it was so in the days of Orpheus, Linus, and Musæus, and would be so again, if it were not that writers prove traitors to themselves. That, in particular, in the days of the first of those three great authors just mentioned, audiences appear to have been perfect models of what audiences should be ; for though, along with the trees and the rocks and the wild creatures which he drew after him to listen to his strains, some serpents doubtless came to hear his music, it does not appear that any one among them ever lifted up *a dissentient voice*. They knew what was due to authors in those days. Now every stock and stone turns into a serpent and has a voice.

That the terms ' Courteous Reader ' and ' Candid Auditors,' as having given rise to a

false notion in those to whom they were applied, as if they conferred upon them some
right, *which they cannot have*, of exercising their
judgments, ought to be utterly banished and
exploded.

These are our distinguishing tenets. To keep
up the memory of the cause in which we suffered, as the ancients sacrificed a goat — a supposed unhealthy animal — to Æsculapius, on our
feast-nights we cut up a goose — an animal typical of *the popular voice* — to the deities of Candour and Patient Hearing. A zealous member
of the society once proposed that we should re-
vive the obsolete luxury of viper-broth ; but
the stomachs of some of the company rising at
the proposition, we lost the benefit of that highly
salutary and *antidotal dish.*

The privilege of admission to our club is
strictly limited to such as have been fairly
damned. A piece that has met with ever so
little applause, that has but languished its night
or two, and then gone out, will never entitle its
author to a seat among us. An exception to
our usual readiness in conferring this privilege
is in the case of a writer who, having been once
condemned, writes again, and becomes candi-
date for a second martyrdom. Simple damnation we hold to be a merit ; but to be twice

damned we adjudge infamous.   Such a one we utterly reject and blackball without a hearing :

The common damned shun his society.

Hoping that your publication of our Regulations may be a means of inviting some more members into our society, I conclude this long letter.

I am, sir, yours,

SEMEL–DAMNATUS.

JOHN KEMBLE AND GODWIN'S
TRAGEDY OF 'ANTONIO.'[1]

THE story of his swallowing opium pills to keep him lively upon the first night of a certain tragedy, we may presume to be a piece of retaliatory pleasantry on the part of the suffering author. But, indeed, John had the art of diffusing a complacent, equable dulness (which you knew not where to quarrel with) over a piece which he did not like, beyond any of his contemporaries. John Kemble had made up his mind early that all the good tragedies which could be written had been written, and he resented any new attempt. His shelves were full. The old standards were scope enough for his ambition. He ranged in them absolute, and ' fair in Otway, full in Shakspeare shone.' He succeeded to the old lawful thrones, and did not care to adventure bottomry with a Sir

---

[1] This essay originally made part of that on the ' Artificial Comedy of Last Century,' as it was first printed in the ' London Magazine ' for 1822. Lamb afterwards omitted it.

Edward Mortimer or any casual speculator that offered.

I remember, too acutely for my peace, the deadly extinguisher which he put upon my friend G.'s ' Antonio.' G., satiate with visions of political justice (possibly not to be realized in our time), or willing to let the sceptical worldlings see that his anticipations of the future did not preclude a warm sympathy for men as they are and have been, wrote a tragedy. He chose a story, affecting, romantic, Spanish ; the plot simple without being naked, the incidents uncommon without being overstrained. Antonio, who gives the name to the piece, is a sensitive young Castilian who in a fit of his country honour immolates his sister.

But I must not anticipate the catastrophe. The play, reader, is extant in choice English, and you will employ a spare half-crown not injudiciously in the quest of it.

The conception was bold, and the *dénouement*, the time and place in which the hero of it existed considered, not much out of keeping ; yet it must be confessed that it required a delicacy of handling, both from the author and the performer, so as not much to shock the prejudices of a modern English audience. G., in my opinion, has done his part. John, who was

in familiar habits with the philosopher, had
undertaken to play Antonio.   Great expectations were formed.   A philosopher's first play
was a new era.   The night arrived.   I was
favoured with a seat in an advantageous box,
between the author and his friend M.   G. sat
cheerful and confident.   In his friend M.'s
looks, who had perused the manuscript, I read
some terror.   Antonio, in the person of John
Philip Kemble, at length appeared, starched
out in a ruff which no one could dispute, and
in most irreproachable mustachios.   John always
dressed   most   provokingly correct   on these
occasions.   The first act swept by, solemn and
silent.   It went off, as G. assured M., exactly
as the opening act of a piece — the *protasis* —
should do.   The cue of the spectators was to
be mute.   The characters were but in their introduction.   The passions and the incidents
would be developed hereafter.   Applause hitherto would be impertinent.   Silent attention
was the effect all-desirable.   Poor M. acqui-
esced, but in his honest, friendly face I could
discern a working which told how much more
acceptable the plaudit of a single hand (however
misplaced) would have been than all this reasoning.   The second act (as in duty bound) rose
a little in interest ; but still John kept his

forces under,—in policy, as G. would have it,—
and the audience were most complacently atten-
tive. The *protasis*, in fact, was scarcely un-
folded. The interest would warm in the next
act, against which a special incident was pro-
vided. M. wiped his cheek, flushed with a
friendly perspiration,—'t is M.'s way of showing
his zeal; ' from every pore of him a perfume
falls.' I honour it above Alexander's. He had
once or twice during this act joined his palms
in a feeble endeavour to elicit a sound; they
emitted a solitary noise without an echo: there
was no deep to answer to his deep. G. repeatedly begged him to be quiet. The third act at
length brought on the scene which was to warm
the piece progressively to the final flaming forth
of the catastrophe. A philosophic calm settled
upon the clear brow of G. as it approached.
The lips of M. quivered. A challenge was held
forth upon the stage, and there was a promise
of a fight. The pit roused themselves on this
extraordinary occasion, and, as their manner is,
seemed disposed to make a ring; when suddenly
Antonio, who was the challenged, turning the
tables upon the hot challenger, Don Gusman
(who, by the way, should have had his sister),
balks his humour, and the pit's reasonable expectation at the same time, with some speeches

out of the new philosophy against duelling. The audience were here fairly caught; their courage was up and on the alert; a few blows, *ding-dong*, as R——s, the dramatist, afterwards expressed it to me, might have done the business, — when their most exquisite moral sense was suddenly called in to assist in the mortifying negation of their own pleasure. They could not applaud for disappointment; they would not condemn for morality's sake. The interest stood stone-still, and John's manner was not at all calculated to unpetrify it. It was Christmas time, and the atmosphere furnished some pretext for asthmatic affections. One began to cough; his neighbour sympathized with him, till a cough became epidemical. But when, from being half-artificial in the pit, the cough got frightfully naturalized among the fictitious persons of the drama, and Antonio himself (albeit it was not set down in the stage directions) seemed more intent upon relieving his own lungs than the distresses of the author and his friends, then G. 'first knew fear,' and, mildly turning to M., intimated that he had not been aware that Mr. Kemble laboured under a cold, and that the performance might possibly have been postponed with advantage for some nights further, — still keeping the same serene countenance, while M. sweated like a bull.

It would be invidious to pursue the fates of this ill-starred evening. In vain did the plot thicken in the scenes that followed, in vain the dialogue was more passionate and stirring, and the progress of the sentiment point more and more clearly to the arduous development which impended. In vain the action was accelerated, while the acting stood still. From the beginning John had taken his stand, — had wound himself up to an even tenure of stately declamation, from which no exigence of dialogue or person could make him swerve for an instant. To dream of his rising with the scene (the common trick of tragedians) was preposterous ; for from the onset he had planted himself, as upon a terrace, on an eminence vastly above the audience, and he kept that sublime level to the end. He looked from his throne of elevated sentiment upon the under-world of spectators with a most sovereign and becoming contempt. There was excellent pathos delivered out to them : an they would receive it, so ; an they would not receive it, so. There was no offence against decorum in all this ; nothing to condemn, to damn ; not an irreverent symptom of a sound was to be heard. The pro-

cession of verbiage stalked on through four
and five acts, no one venturing to predict what
would come of it, when, towards the winding up
of the latter, Antonio, with an irrelevancy that
seemed to stagger Elvira herself, — for she had
been coolly arguing the point of honour with
him, — suddenly whips out a poniard and stabs
his sister to the heart.   The effect was as if a
murder had been committed in cold blood.
The whole house rose up in clamorous indignation, demanding justice.   The feeling rose far
above hisses.   I believe at that instant, if they
could have got him, they would have torn the
unfortunate author to pieces.   Not that the act
itself was so exorbitant, or of a complexion
different from what they themselves would have
applauded upon another occasion in a Brutus
or an Appius ; but for want of attending to Antonio's *words*, which palpably led to the expectation of no less dire an event, instead of
being seduced by his *manner*, which seemed to
promise a sleep of a less alarming nature than
it was his cue to inflict upon Elvira, they found
themselves betrayed into an accompliceship of
murder, a perfect misprision of parricide, while
they dreamed of nothing less.

M., I believe, was the only person who
suffered acutely from the failure ; for G. thence-

forward, with a serenity unattainable but by the true philosophy, abandoning a precarious popularity, retired into his fasthold of speculation, — the drama in which the world was to be his tiring-room, and remote posterity his applauding spectators at once and actors.

STAGE ILLUSION.

A PLAY is said to be well or ill acted, in proportion to the scenical illusion produced. Whether such illusion can in any case be perfect, is not the question. The nearest approach to it, we are told, is when the actor appears wholly unconscious of the presence of spectators. In tragedy — in all which is to affect the feelings — this undivided attention to his stage business seems indispensable. Yet it is, in fact, dispensed with every day by our cleverest tragedians ; and while these references to an audience, in the shape of rant or sentiment, are not too frequent or palpable, a sufficient quantity of illusion for the purposes of dramatic interest may be said to be produced in spite of them. But, tragedy apart, it may be inquired whether, in certain characters in comedy, especially those which are a little extravagant, or which involve some notion repugnant to the moral sense, it is not a proof of the highest skill in the comedian when, without absolutely appealing to an audience, he keeps up a tacit understanding with them, and makes them, unconsciously to themselves, a party in the scene.   The utmost nicety is required in the mode of doing this ; but we speak only of the great artists in the profession.

The most mortifying infirmity in human nature to feel in ourselves or to contemplate in another is perhaps cowardice.   To see a coward *done to the life* upon a stage would produce anything but mirth.   Yet we most of us remember Jack Bannister's cowards.   Could anything be more agreeable, more pleasant ? We loved the rogues.   How was this effected but by the exquisite art of the actor in a perpetual sub-insinuation to us, the spectators, even in the extremity of the shaking fit, that he was not half such a coward as we took him for ? We saw all the common symptoms of the malady upon him, — the quivering lip, the cowering knees, the teeth chattering, — and could have sworn 'that man was frightened.'   But we forgot all the while — or kept it almost a secret to ourselves — that he never once lost his self-possession ; that he let out, by a thousand droll looks and gestures, — meant at *us*, and not at all supposed to be visible to his fellows in the scene, — that his confidence in his own resources

had never once deserted him. Was this a
genuine picture of a coward, or not rather a
likeness which the clever artist contrived to
palm upon us instead of an original, while we
secretly connived at the delusion for the purpose of greater pleasure than a more genuine
counterfeiting of the imbecility, helplessness,
and utter self-desertion which we know to be
concomitants of cowardice in real life could
have given us?

Why are misers so hateful in the world and
so endurable on the stage, but because the
skilful actor, by a sort of subreference, rather
than direct appeal to us, disarms the character
of a great deal of its odiousness, by seeming to
engage *our* compassion for the insecure tenure
by which he holds his money-bags and parch-
ments? By this subtle vent half of the hate-
fulness of the character — the self-closeness
with which in real life it coils itself up from the
sympathies of men — evaporates. The miser
becomes sympathetic ; *i. e.*, is no genuine miser.
Here again a diverting likeness is substituted
for a very disagreeable reality.

Spleen, irritability, the pitiable infirmities of
old men, which produce only pain to behold in
the realities, counterfeited upon a stage divert
not altogether for the comic appendages to

them, but in part from an inner conviction that
they are *being acted* before us ; that a likeness
only is going on, and not the thing itself. They
please by being done under the life, or beside
it, not *to the life.* When Gattie acts an old
man, is he angry indeed ? or only a pleasant
counterfeit, just enough of a likeness to recognize, without pressing upon us the uneasy sense
of a reality ?

Comedians, paradoxical as it may seem, may
be too natural.   It was the case with a late
actor.   Nothing could be more earnest or true
than the manner of Mr. Emery ; this told ex-
cellently in his Tyke, and characters of a tragic
cast.   But when he carried the same rigid ex-
clusiveness of attention to the stage business,
and wilful blindness and oblivion of everything
before the curtain into his comedy, it produced
a harsh and dissonant effect.   He was out of
keeping with the rest of the *dramatis personæ.*
There was as little link between him and them
as betwixt himself and the audience.   He was
a third estate, — dry, repulsive, and unsocial to
all.   Individually considered, his execution was
masterly.   But comedy is not this unbending
thing, — for this reason, that the same degree of
credibility is not required of it as to serious
scenes. The degrees of credibility demanded

to the two things may be illustrated by the different sort of truth which we expect when a man tells us a mournful or a merry story. If we suspect the former of falsehood in any one tittle, we reject it altogether. Our tears refuse to flow at a suspected imposition. But the teller of a mirthful tale has latitude allowed him. We are content with less than absolute truth. 'T is the same with dramatic illusion. We confess we love in comedy to see an audience naturalized behind the scenes, — taken into the interest of the drama, welcomed as bystanders, however. There is something ungracious in a comic actor holding himself aloof from all participation or concern with those who are come to be diverted by him. Macbeth must see the dagger, and no ear but his own be told of it; but an old fool in farce may think he *sees something*, and by conscious words and looks express it, as plainly as he can speak, to pit, box, and gallery. When an impertinent in tragedy, an Osric, for instance, breaks in upon the serious passions of the scene, we approve of the contempt with which he is treated. But when the pleasant impertinent of comedy, in a piece purely meant to give delight and raise mirth out of whimsical perplexities, worries the studious man with taking up his leisure, or making

K

his house his home, the same sort of contempt expressed (however *natural*) would destroy the balance of delight in the spectators.   To make the intrusion comic, the actor who plays the annoyed man must a little desert nature ; he must, in short, be thinking of the audience, and express only so much dissatisfaction and peevishness as is consistent with the pleasure of comedy.   In other words, his perplexity must seem half put on.   If he repel the intruder with the sober, set face of a man in earnest, and more especially if he deliver his expostulations in a tone which in the world must necessarily provoke a duel, his real-life manner will destroy the whimsical and purely dramatic existence of the other character (which to render it comic demands an antagonist comicality on the part of the character opposed to it), and convert what was meant for mirth, rather than belief, into a downright piece of impertinence indeed, which would raise no diversion in us, but rather stir pain, to see inflicted in earnest upon any worthy person.   A very judicious actor (in most of his parts) seems to have fallen into an error of this sort in his playing with Mr. Wrench in the fàrce of ' Free and Easy.'

Many instances would be tedious ; these may suffice to show that comic acting at least does not always demand from the performer that strict abstraction from all reference to an audience which is exacted of it, but that in some cases a sort of compromise may take place, and all the purposes of dramatic delight be attained by a judicious understanding, not too openly announced, between the ladies and gentlemen on both sides of the curtain.

ON THE ARTIFICIAL COMEDY OF
THE LAST CENTURY.

THE artificial Comedy, or Comedy of manners, is quite extinct on our stage. Congreve and Farquhar show their heads once in
seven years only, to be exploded and put down
instantly ; the times cannot bear them. Is it
for a few wild speeches, an occasional license
of dialogue ? I think not altogether. The
business of their dramatic characters will not
stand the moral test. We screw everything up
to that. Idle gallantry in a fiction, a dream,
the passing pageant of an evening, startles us in
the same way as the alarming indications of
profligacy in a son or ward in real life should
startle a parent or guardian. We have no such
middle emotions as dramatic interests left. We
see a stage libertine playing his loose pranks
of two hours' duration, and of no after consequence, with the severe eyes which inspect
real vices with their bearings upon two worlds.
We are spectators to a plot or intrigue (not re-
ducible in life to the point of strict morality),

and take it all for truth. We substitute a real
for a dramatic person, and judge him accordingly. We try him in our courts, from which
there is no appeal to the *dramatis personæ*, his
peers. We have been spoiled with, not sentimental comedy, but a tyrant far more pernicious to our pleasures which has succeeded to
it, — the exclusive and all-devouring drama of
common life, where the moral point is everything, where, instead of the fictitious, half-
believed personages of the stage (the phantoms
of old comedy), we recognize ourselves, our
brothers, aunts, kinsfolk, allies, patrons, enemies, — the same as in life, — with an interest
in what is going on so hearty and substantial
that we cannot afford our moral judgment, in its
deepest and most vital results, to compromise
or slumber for a moment. What is *there* trans-
acting, by no modification is made to affect us
in any other manner than the same events or
characters would do in our relationships of life.
We carry our fire-side concerns to the theatre
with us. We do not go thither, like our ancestors, to escape from the pressure of reality so
much as to confirm our experience of it, — to
make assurance double, and take a bond of fate.
We must live our toilsome lives twice over, as
it was the mournful privilege of Ulysses to de-

scend twice to the shades.   All that neutral
ground of character which stood between vice
and virtue, or which in fact was indifferent to
neither, where neither properly was called in
question, that happy breathing-place from the
burthen of a perpetual moral questioning, — the
sanctuary and quiet Alsatia of hunted casuistry
— is broken up and disfranchised, as injurious
to the interests of society.   The privileges of
the place are taken away by law.   We dare
not dally with images, or names, of wrong.
We bark like foolish dogs at shadows.   We
dread infection from the scenic representation
of disorder, and fear a painted pustule.   In our
anxiety that our morality should not take cold,
we wrap it up in a great blanket surtout of
precaution against the breeze and sunshine.

I confess for myself that (with no great de-
linquencies to answer for) I am glad for a season
to take an airing beyond the diocese of the
strict conscience, — not to live always in the
precincts of the law courts, but now and then,
for a dream-while or so, to imagine a world
with no meddling restrictions, to get into recesses whither the hunter cannot follow me, —

> Secret shades
> Of woody Ida's inmost grove,
> While yet there was no fear of Jove.

I come back to my cage and my restraint the
fresher and more healthy for it. I wear my
shackles more contentedly for having respired
the breath of an imaginary freedom. I do not
know how it is with others, but I feel the better
always for the perusal of one of Congreve's —
nay, why should I not add even of Wycherley's ?
— comedies. I am the gayer at least for it ;
and I could never connect those sports of a
witty fancy in any shape with any result to be
drawn from them to imitation in real life. They
are a world of themselves almost as much as
fairyland. Take one of their characters, male
or female (with few exceptions they are alike),
and place it in a modern play, and my virtuous indignation shall rise against the profli-
gate wretch as warmly as the Catos of the pit
could desire, because in a modern play I am to
judge of the right and the wrong. The standard
of *police* is the measure of *political justice.*
The atmosphere will blight it ; it cannot live
here. It has got into a moral world, where it
has no business, from which it must needs fall
headlong, — as dizzy and incapable of making a
stand as a Swedenborgian bad spirit that has
wandered unawares into the sphere of one of
his Good Men or Angels. But in its own
world do we feel the creature is so very bad ?

The Fainalls and the Mirabels, the Dorimants
and the Lady Touchwoods, in their own sphere,
do not offend my moral sense ; in fact, they do
not appeal to it at all.   They seem engaged in
their proper element.   They break through no
laws or conscientious restraints ; they know
of none.   They have got out of Christendom
into the land — what shall I call it ? — of cuck-
oldry, — the Utopia of gallantry, where pleasure
is duty, and the manners perfect freedom.   It
is altogether a speculative scene of things, which
has no reference whatever to the world that is.
No good person can be justly offended as a
spectator, because no good person suffers on
the stage.   Judged morally, every character in
these plays — the few exceptions only are *mistakes* — is alike essentially vain and worthless.
The great art of Congreve is especially shown
in this, that he has entirely excluded from his
scenes, — some little generosities in the part of
Angelica perhaps excepted, — not only anything
like a faultless character, but any pretensions to
goodness or good feelings whatsoever.   Whether
he did this designedly or instinctively, the
effect is as happy as the design (if design) was
bold.   I used to wonder at the strange power
which his ' Way of the World ' in particular possesses of interesting you all along in the pursuits

of characters for whom you absolutely care nothing, — for you neither hate nor love his personages, — and I think it is owing to this very indifference for any that you endure the whole. He has spread a privation of moral light, I will call it, rather than by the ugly name of palpable darkness, over his creations; and his shadows flit before you without distinction or preference. Had he introduced a good character, a single gush of moral feeling, a revulsion of the judgment to actual life and actual duties, the impertinent Goshen would have only lighted to the discovery of deformities which now are none, because we think them none.

Translated into real life, the characters of his and his friend Wycherley's dramas are profligates and strumpets; the business of their brief existence the undivided pursuit of lawless gallantry. No other spring of action or possible motive of conduct is recognized, — principles which, universally acted upon, must reduce this frame of things to a chaos. But we do them wrong in so translating them. No such effects are produced, in *their* world. When we are among them, we are amongst a chaotic people. We are not to judge them by our usages. No reverend institutions are insulted by their proceedings, for they have none among them. No peace of families is violated, for no family ties exist among them. No purity of the marriage bed is stained, for none is supposed to have a being. No deep affections are disquieted, no holy wedlock bands are snapped asunder, for affection's depth and wedded faith are not of the growth of that soil. There is neither right nor wrong, gratitude or its opposite, claim or duty, paternity or sonship. Of what consequence is it to Virtue, or how is she at all concerned about it, whether Sir Simon or Dapperwit steal away Miss Martha, or who is the father of Lord Froth's or Sir Paul Pliant's children?

The whole is a passing pageant, where we should sit as unconcerned at the issues, for life or death, as at the battle of the frogs and mice. But, like Don Quixote, we take part against the puppets, and quite as impertinently. We dare not contemplate an Atlantis, a scheme, out of which our coxcombical moral sense is for a little transitory ease excluded. We have not the courage to imagine a state of things for which there is neither reward nor punishment. We cling to the painful necessities of shame and blame. We would indict our very dreams.

Amidst the mortifying circumstances attendant upon growing old, it is something to have seen the 'School for Scandal' in its glory. This comedy grew out of Congreve and Wycherley, but gathered some allays of the sentimental comedy which followed theirs. It is impossible that it should be now *acted*, though it continues, at long intervals, to be announced in the bills. Its hero, when Palmer played it, at least, was Joseph Surface. When I remember the gay boldness, the graceful, solemn plausibility, the measured step, the insinuating voice, — to express it in a word, the downright *acted* villainy of the part, so different from the pressure of conscious, actual wickedness, the hypocritical assumption of hypocrisy, — which made Jack so deservedly a favourite in that character, I must needs conclude the present generation of playgoers more virtuous than myself, or more dense. I freely confess that he divided the palm with me with his better brother, — that, in fact, I liked him quite as well. Not but there are passages, — like that, for instance, where Joseph is made to refuse a pittance to a poor relation, — incongruities, which Sheridan was forced upon by the attempt to join the artificial with the sentimental comedy, either of which must destroy the other ; but over these obstructions Jack's manner floated him so lightly that a refusal from him no more shocked you than the easy compliance

of Charles gave you in reality any pleasure, —
you got over the paltry question as quickly as
you could, to get back into the regions of pure
comedy, where no cold moral reigns. The
highly artificial manner of Palmer in this character counteracted every disagreeable impression
which you might have received from the contrast, supposing them real, between the two
brothers. You did not believe in Joseph with
the same faith with which you believed in
Charles. The latter was a pleasant reality, the
former a no less pleasant poetical foil to it.
The comedy, I have said, is incongruous, — a
mixture of Congreve with sentimental incom-
patibilities; the gaiety upon the whole is buoyant, but it required the consummate art of
Palmer to reconcile the discordant elements.

A player with Jack's talents, if we had one
now, would not dare to do the part in the same
manner. He would instinctively avoid every
turn which might tend to unrealize, and so to
make the character fascinating. He must take
his cue from his spectators, who would expect a
bad man and a good man as rigidly opposed to
each other as the deathbeds of those geniuses
are contrasted in the prints, which, I am sorry
to say, have disappeared from the windows of
my old friend Carrington Bowles, of St. Paul's

Churchyard memory, — an exhibition as venerable as the adjacent cathedral, and almost coeval, — of the bad and good man at the hour of death ; where the ghastly apprehensions of the former (and truly the grim phantom with his reality of a toasting-fork is not to be despised) so finely contrast with the meek, complacent kissing of the rod, taking it in like honey and butter, with which the latter submits to the scythe of the gentle bleeder, Time, who wields his lancet with the apprehensive finger of a popular young ladies' surgeon. What flesh, like loving grass, would not covet to meet half-way the stroke of such a delicate mower ? John Palmer was twice an actor in this exquisite part. He was playing to you all the while that he was playing upon Sir Peter and his lady. You had the first intimation of a sentiment before it was on his lips. His altered voice was meant to you, and you were to suppose that his fictitious co-flutterers on the stage perceived nothing at all of it. What was it to you if that half reality, the husband, was overreached by the puppetry, or the thin thing (Lady Teazle's reputation) was persuaded it was dying of a plethory ? The fortunes of Othello and Desdemona were not concerned in it. Poor Jack has passed from the stage in good time, that he did not live to

this our age of seriousness. The pleasant old
Teazle *King*, too, is gone in good time. His
manner would scarce have passed current in our
day. We must love or hate, acquit or condemn,
censure or pity, exert our detestable coxcombry
of moral judgment upon everything. Joseph
Surface, to go down now, must be a downright
revolting villain, — no compromise ; his first
appearance must shock and give horror ; his
specious plausibilities, which the pleasurable faculties of our fathers welcomed with such hearty
greetings, knowing that no harm (dramatic
harm even) could come or was meant to come of
them, must inspire a cold and killing aversion.
Charles (the real canting person of the scene, —
for the hypocrisy of Joseph has its ulterior legitimate ends ; but his brother's professions of a
good heart centre in downright self-satisfaction)
must be *loved*, and Joseph *hated*. To balance
one disagreeable reality with another, Sir Peter
Teazle must be no longer the comic idea of a
fretful old bachelor bridegroom whose teasings
(while King acted it) were evidently as much
played off at you as they were meant to concern anybody on the stage, he must be a real
person, capable in law of sustaining an injury, —
a person towards whom duties are to be acknowledged, the genuine *crim. con.* antagonist

of the villainous seducer Joseph. To realize him more, his sufferings under his unfortunate match must have the downright pungency of life, must (or should) make you, not mirthful, but uncomfortable, just as the same predicament would move you in a neighbour or old friend.

The delicious scenes which give the play its name and zest must affect you in the same serious manner as if you heard the reputation of a dear female friend attacked in your real presence. Crabtree and Sir Benjamin, those poor snakes that live but in the sunshine of your mirth, must be ripened by this hot-bed process of realization into asps or amphisbænas, and Mrs. Candour — oh, frightful ! — become a hooded serpent. Oh, who that remembers Parsons and Dodd — the wasp and butterfly of the ' School for Scandal ' — in those two characters, and charming, natural Miss Pope, the perfect gentlewoman, as distinguished from the fine lady of comedy, in this latter part, would forego the true scenic delight, the escape from life, the oblivion of consequences, the holiday barring out of the pedant Reflection, those Saturnalia of two or three brief hours well won from the world, to sit instead at one of our modern plays, to have his coward conscience (that, forsooth, must not be left for a moment) stimulated with per-

petual appeals, dulled rather, and blunted, as a
faculty without repose must be, and his moral
vanity pampered with images of notional justice,
notional beneficence, lives saved without the
spectator's risk, and fortunes given away that
cost the author nothing?

No piece was, perhaps, ever so completely
cast in all its parts as this *manager's comedy*.
Miss Farren had succeeded to Mrs. Abington
in Lady Teazle, and Smith, the original Charles,
had retired when I first saw it. The rest of the
characters, with very slight exceptions, remained. I remember it was then the fashion to
cry down John Kemble, who took the part of
Charles after Smith; but I thought very un-
justly. Smith, I fancy, was more airy, and
took the eye with a certain gaiety of person.
He brought with him no sombre recollections
of tragedy. He had not to expiate the fault of
having pleased beforehand in lofty declamation.
He had no sins of Hamlet or of Richard to
atone for. His failure in these parts was a
passport to success in one of so opposite a
tendency. But as far as I could judge, the
weighty sense of Kemble made up for more
personal incapacity than he had to answer for.
His harshest tones in this part came steeped
and dulcified in good humour. He made his

defects a grace. His exact declamatory manner, as he managed it, only served to convey the points of his dialogue with more precision ; it seemed to head the shafts to carry them deeper. Not one of his sparkling sentences was lost. I remember minutely how he delivered each in succession, and cannot by any effort imagine how any of them could be altered for the better. No man could deliver brilliant dialogue — the dialogue of Congreve or of Wycherley — because none understood it half so well as John Kemble. His Valentine, in ' Love for Love,' was, to my recollection, faultless. He flagged sometimes in the intervals of tragic passion. He would slumber over the level parts of an heroic character. His Macbeth has been known to nod. But he always seemed to me to be particularly alive to pointed and witty dialogue. The relaxing levities of tragedy have not been touched by any since him; the playful, court-bred spirit in which he condescended to the players in Hamlet, the sportive relief which he threw into the darker shades of Richard, disappeared with him. He had his sluggish moods, his torpors ; but they were the halting-stones and resting-place of his tragedy, — politic savings and fetches of the breath, husbandry of the lungs, where Nature pointed him to be an

L

economist, rather, I think, than errors of the judgment.   They were, at worst, less painful than the eternal tormenting, unappeasable vigilance, the ' lidless dragon eyes,' of present fashionable tragedy.

ON THE TRAGEDIES OF
SHAKSPEARE,

CONSIDERED WITH REFERENCE TO THEIR FITNESS
FOR STAGE REPRESENTATION.

TAKING a turn the other day in the Abbey, I was struck with the affected attitude of a figure which I do not remember to have seen before, and which upon examination proved to be a whole-length of the celebrated Mr. Garrick. Though I would not go so far with some good Catholics abroad as to shut players altogether out of consecrated ground, yet I own I was not a little scandalized at the introduction of theatrical airs and gestures into a place set apart to remind us of the saddest realities. Going nearer, I found inscribed under this harlequin figure the following lines : —

> To paint fair Nature, by divine command,
> Her magic pencil in his glowing hand,
> A Shakspeare rose ; then, to expand his fame
> Wide o'er this breathing world, a Garrick came.

> Though sunk in death the forms the Poet drew,
> The Actor's genius made them breathe anew;
> Though, like the bard himself, in night they lay,
> Immortal Garrick called them back to-day.
> And till Eternity with power sublime
> Shall mark the mortal hour of hoary Time,
> Shakspeare and Garrick like twin-stars shall shine,
> And earth irradiate with a beam divine.

It would be an insult to my readers' under-standings to attempt anything like a criticism on this farrago of false thoughts and nonsense. But the reflection it led me into was a kind of wonder how, from the days of the actor here celebrated to our own, it should have been the fashion to compliment every performer in his turn that has had the luck to please the town in any of the great characters of Shakspeare, with a notion of possessing a *mind congenial with the poet's;* how people should come thus unac-countably to confound the power of originating poetical images and conceptions with the faculty of being able to read or recite the same when put into words ; [1] or what connection that abso-

---

[1] It is observable that we fall into this confusion only in *dramatic* recitations. We never dream that the gen-tleman who reads Lucretius in public with great applause is therefore a great poet and philosopher, nor do we find that Tom Davies, the bookseller, who is recorded to have recited the 'Paradise Lost' better than any man in England in his day (though I cannot help thinking there must be

lute mastery over the heart and soul of man, which a great dramatic poet possesses, has with those low tricks upon the eye and ear, which a player by observing a few general effects, which some common passion, as grief, anger, etc., usually has upon the gestures and exterior, can easily compass. To know the internal workings and movements of a great mind, of an Othello or a Hamlet, for instance ; the *when* and the *why* and the *how far* they should be moved ; to what pitch a passion is becoming ; to give the reins and to pull in the curb exactly at the moment when the drawing in or the slacking is most graceful, — seems to demand a reach of intellect of a vastly different extent from that which is employed upon the bare imitation of the signs of these passions in the countenance or gesture, which signs are usually observed to be most lively and emphatic in the weaker sort of minds, and which signs can, after all, but indicate some passion, as I said before, anger, or grief generally. But of the motives and grounds of the passion, wherein it differs from the same passion in low and vulgar natures, of these the actor can give no more idea by his face or gesture than the eye (without a meta-

some mistake in this tradition) was therefore, by his intimate friends, set upon a level with Milton.

phor) can speak, or the muscles utter intelligible sounds.   But such is the instantaneous nature of the impressions which we take in at the eye and ear at a playhouse, compared with the slow apprehension oftentimes of the understanding in reading, that we are apt not only to sink the playwriter in the consideration which we pay to the actor, but even to identify in our minds in a perverse manner, the actor with the character which he represents.   It is difficult for a frequent play-goer to disembarrass the idea of Hamlet from the person and voice of Mr. K. We speak of Lady Macbeth, while we are in reality thinking of Mrs. S. ' Nor is this confusion incidental alone to unlettered persons, who, not possessing the advantage of reading, are necessarily dependent upon the stage-player for all the pleasure which they can receive from the drama, and to whom the very idea of *what an author is* cannot be made comprehensible without some pain and perplexity of mind.   The error is one from which persons otherwise not meanly lettered, find it almost impossible to extricate themselves.

Never let me be so ungrateful as to forget the very high degree of satisfaction which I received some years back from seeing for the first time a tragedy of Shakspeare performed,

in which these two great performers sustained
the principal parts. It seemed to embody and
realize conceptions which had hitherto assumed
no distinct shape. But dearly do we pay all
our life afterwards for this juvenile pleasure,
this sense of distinctness. When the novelty is
past, we find to our cost that, instead of realiz-
ing an idea, we have only materialized and
brought down a fine vision to the standard of
flesh and blood. We have let go a dream, in
quest of an unattainable substance.

How cruelly this operates upon the mind,
to have its free conceptions thus cramped and
pressed down to the measure of a strait-lacing
actuality, may be judged from that delightful
sensation of freshness with which we turn to
those plays of Shakspeare which have escaped
being performed, and to those passages in the
acting plays of the same writer which have
happily been left out in the performance. How
far the very custom of hearing anything *spouted*,
withers and blows upon a fine passage, may be
seen in those speeches from ' Henry the Fifth,'
etc., which are current in the mouths of school-
boys from their being to be found in ' Enfield
Speakers ' and such kind of books. I confess
myself utterly unable to appreciate that celebrated soliloquy in ' Hamlet,' beginning ' To be,

or not to be,' or to tell whether it be good, bad, or indifferent, it has been so handled and pawed about by declamatory boys and men, and torn so inhumanly from its living place and principle of continuity in the play, till it is become to me a perfect dead member.

It may seem a paradox, but I cannot help being of opinion that the plays of Shakspeare are less calculated for performance on a stage than those of almost any other dramatist whatever. Their distinguished excellence is a reason that they should be so ; there is so much in them which comes not under the province of acting, with which eye and tone and gesture have nothing to do.

The glory of the scenic art is to personate passion and the turns of passion ; and the more coarse and palpable the passion is, the more hold upon the eyes and ears of the spectators the performer obviously possesses.   For this reason, scolding scenes, scenes where two persons talk themselves into a fit of fury, and then in a surprising manner talk themselves out of it again, have always been the most popular upon our stage.   And the reason is plain, because the spectators are here most palpably appealed to, — they are the proper judges in this war of words; they are the legitimate ring that should be formed round such 'intellectual prize-fighters.' Talking is the direct object of the imitation here. But in the best dramas, and in Shakspeare above all, how obvious it is that the form of *speaking*, whether it be in soliloquy or dialogue, is only a medium, and often a highly-artificial one, for putting the reader or spectator into possession of that knowledge of the inner structure and workings of mind in a character, which he could otherwise never have arrived at *in that form of composition* by any gift short of intuition. We do here as we do with novels written in the *epistolary form.* How many improprieties, perfect solecisms, in letter-writing do we put up with in ' Clarissa ' and other books for the sake of the delight which that form upon the whole gives us !

But the practice of stage representation reduces everything to a controversy of elocution. Every character, from the boisterous blasphemings of Bajazet to the shrinking timidity of womanhood, must play the orator. The love-dialogues of ' Romeo and Juliet,' those silver-sweet sounds of lovers' tongues by night ; the more intimate and sacred sweetness of nuptial colloquy between an Othello or a Posthumus with their married wives ; all those delicacies which are so delightful in the reading, as when

we read of those youthful dalliances in
Paradise, —

> As beseemed
> Fair couple linked in happy nuptial league,
> Alone, —

by the inherent fault of stage representation,
how are these things sullied and turned from
their very nature by being exposed to a large
assembly; when such speeches as Imogen
addresses to her lord come drawling out of the
mouth of a hired actress, whose courtship,
though nominally addressed to the personated
Posthumus, is manifestly aimed at the spectators, who are to judge of her endearments and
her returns of love.

The character of Hamlet is perhaps that by
which, since the days of Betterton, a succession of popular performers have had the greatest
ambition to distinguish themselves. The length
of the part may be one of their reasons. But
for the character itself, we find it in a play,
and therefore we judge it a fit subject of dramatic representation. The play itself abounds
in maxims and reflections beyond any other,
and therefore we consider it as a proper vehicle
for conveying moral instruction. But Hamlet
himself, — what does he suffer meanwhile by
being dragged forth as a public schoolmaster

to give lectures to the crowd ! Why, nine
parts in ten of what Hamlet does are transac-
tions between himself and his moral sense ; they
are the effusions of his solitary musings, which
he retires to holes and corners and the most
sequestered parts of the palace to pour forth, —
or rather, they are the silent meditations with
which his bosom is bursting, reduced to *words* for
the sake of the reader, who must else remain ignorant of what is passing there. These profound
sorrows, these light-and-noise-abhorring rumina-
tions, which the tongue scarce dares utter to
deaf walls and chambers, how can they be
represented by a gesticulating actor who comes
and mouths them out before an audience, making four hundred people his confidants at once ?
I say not that it is the fault of the actor so to
do ; he must pronounce them *ore rotundo*, he
must accompany them with his eye, he must
insinuate them into his auditory by some trick
of eye, tone, or gesture, or he fails. *He must
be thinking all the while of his appearance,
because he knows that all the while the spectators are judging of it.* And this is the way
to represent the shy, negligent, retiring
Hamlet !

It is true that there is no other mode of conveying a vast quantity of thought and feeling to

a great portion of the audience, who otherwise
would never learn it for themselves by reading,
and the intellectual acquisition gained this way
may, for aught I know, be inestimable ; but I
am not arguing that ' Hamlet ' should not be
acted, but how much ' Hamlet ' is made another
thing by being acted.   I have heard much of
the wonders which Garrick performed in this
part ; but as I never saw him, I must have leave
to doubt whether the representation of such a
character came within the province of his art.
Those who tell me of him, speak of his eye, of
the magic of his eye, and of his commanding
voice, — physical properties vastly desirable in
an actor, and without which he can never insinuate meaning into an auditory.   But what have
they to do with Hamlet ? What have they to do
with intellect ?   In fact, the things aimed at in
theatrical representation are to arrest the spectator's eye upon the form and the gesture, and
so to gain a more favourable hearing to what is
spoken.   It is not what the character is, but how
he looks ; not what he says, but how he speaks
it.   I see no reason to think that if the play of
' Hamlet ' were written over again by some such
writer as Banks or Lillo, retaining the process
of the story, but totally omitting all the poetry
of it, all the divine features of Shakspeare, his

stupendous intellect, and only taking care to give us enough of passionate dialogue, which Banks or Lillo were never at a loss to furnish, — I see not how the effect could be much different upon an audience, nor how the actor has it in his power to represent Shakspeare to us differently from his representation of Banks or Lillo. Hamlet would still be a youthful accomplished prince, and must be gracefully personated; he might be puzzled in his mind, wavering in his conduct, seemingly cruel to Ophelia; he might see a ghost, and start at it, and address it kindly when he found it to be his father, — all this in the poorest and most homely language of the servilest creeper after nature that ever consulted the palate of an audience, without troubling Shakspeare for the matter; and I see not but there would be room for all the power which an actor has to display itself. All the passions and changes of passion might remain, for those are much less difficult to write or act than is thought, — it is a trick easy to be attained, it is but rising or falling a note or two in the voice, a whisper, with a significant foreboding look to announce its approach; and so contagious the counterfeit appearance of any emotion is, that let the words be what they will, the look and tone shall carry it off and make it pass for deep skill in the passions.

It is common for people to talk of Shakspeare's plays being *so natural* that everybody can understand him. They are natural indeed, they are grounded deep in nature, — so deep that the depth of them lies out of the reach of most of us. You shall hear the same persons say that 'George Barnwell' is very natural, and 'Othello' is very natural, that they are both very deep ; and to them they are the same kind of thing. At the one they sit and shed tears because a good sort of young man is tempted by a naughty woman to commit *a trifling peccadillo*, the murder of an uncle or so,[1] that is all,

[1] If this note could hope to meet the eye of any of the managers, I would entreat and beg of them, in the name of both the galleries, that this insult upon the morality of the common people of London should cease to be eternally repeated in the holiday weeks. Why are the 'prentices of this famous and well-governed city, instead of an amusement, to be treated over and over again with a nauseous sermon of George Barnwell? Why *at the end of their vistas* are we to place the *gallows?* Were I an uncle, I should not much like a nephew of mine to have such an example placed before his eyes. It is really making uncle-murder too trivial to exhibit it as done upon such slight motives ; it is attributing too much to such characters as Millwood; it is putting things into the heads of good young men which they would never other-

and so comes to an untimely end, which is *so moving;* and at the other, because a blackamoor in a fit of jealousy kills his innocent white wife, — and the odds are that ninety-nine out of a hundred would willingly behold the same catastrophe happen to both the heroes, and have thought the rope more due to Othello than to Barnwell. For of the texture of Othello's mind, the inward construction marvellously laid open, with all its strengths and weaknesses, its heroic confidences and its human misgivings, its agonies of hate springing from the depths of love, they see no more than the spectators at a cheaper rate, who pay their pennies apiece to look through the man's telescope in Leicester Fields, see into the inward plot and topography of the moon. Some dim thing or other they see, — they see an actor personating a passion, of grief or anger, for instance, and they recognize it as a copy of the usual external effects of such passions, or at least as being true to *that symbol of the emotion which passes current at the theatre for it*; for it is often no more than that. But of the grounds of the passion, its correspondence to a great or heroic nature,

wise have dreamed of. Uncles that think anything of their lives should fairly petition the Chamberlain against it.

which is the only worthy object of tragedy;
that common auditors know anything of this, or
can have any such notions dinned into them
by the mere strength of an actor's lungs, —
that apprehensions foreign to them should be
thus infused into them by storm, I can
neither believe, nor understand how it can be
possible.

We talk of Shakspeare's admirable observation of life, when we should feel that not from
a petty inquisition into those cheap and every-
day characters which surrounded him, as they
surround us, but from his own mind, which was,
to borrow a phrase of Ben Jonson's, the very
'sphere of humanity,' he fetched those images
of virtue and of knowledge, of which every one
of us, recognizing a part, think we comprehend
in our natures the whole, and oftentimes mistake the powers which he positively creates in
us for nothing more than indigenous faculties
of our own minds, which only waited the application of corresponding virtues in him to return
a full and clear echo of the same.

To return to Hamlet. Among the distinguishing features of that wonderful character,
one of the most interesting (yet painful) is that
soreness of mind which makes him treat the
intrusions of Polonius with harshness, and that

asperity which he puts on in his interviews with Ophelia. These tokens of an unhinged mind (if they be not mixed in the latter case with a profound artifice of love, to alienate Ophelia by affected discourtesies, so to prepare her mind for the breaking off of that loving inter‑ course, which can no longer find a place amidst business so serious as that which he has to do) are parts of his character, which, to reconcile with our admiration of Hamlet, the most patient consideration of his situation is no more than necessary ; they are what we *forgive afterwards*, and explain by the whole of his character, but *at the time* they are harsh and unpleasant. Yet such is the actor's necessity of giving strong blows to the audience that I have never seen a player in this character who did not exagger‑ ate and strain to the utmost these ambiguous features, — these temporary deformities in the character. They make him express a vulgar scorn at Polonius which utterly degrades his gentility, and which no explanation can render palatable ; they make him show contempt and curl up the nose at Ophelia's father, — con‑ tempt in its very grossest and most hateful form ; but they get applause by it : it is natural, people say, — that is, the words are scornful, and the actor expresses scorn, and that they

M

can judge of ; but why so much scorn, and of
that sort, they never think of asking.

So to Ophelia. All the Hamlets that I have
ever seen, rant and rave at her as if she had
committed some great crime, and the audience
are highly pleased, because the words of the
part are satirical, and they are enforced by the
strongest expression of satirical indignation of
which the face and voice are capable. But
then, whether Hamlet is likely to have put on
such brutal appearances to a lady whom he
loved so dearly, is never thought on. The
truth is, that in all such deep affections as had
subsisted between Hamlet and Ophelia, there
is a stock of *supererogatory love* (if I may venture to use the expression), which in any great
grief of heart, especially where that which
preys upon the mind cannot be communicated,
confers a kind of indulgence upon the grieved
party to express itself, even to its heart's dear-
est object, in the language of a temporary
alienation ; but it is not alienation, it is a distraction purely, and so it always makes itself to be
felt by that object : it is not anger, but grief
assuming the appearance of anger, — love
awkwardly counterfeiting hate, as sweet countenances when they try to frown. But such stern-
ness and fierce disgust as Hamlet is made to

show, is no counterfeit, but the real face of absolute aversion, of irreconcilable alienation. It
may be said he puts on the madman ; but then
he should only so far put on this counterfeit
lunacy as his own real distraction will give him
leave ; that is, imcompletely, imperfectly, not
in that confirmed, practised way, like a master
of his art, or, as Dame Quickly would say,
' like one of those harlotry players.'

I mean no disrespect to any actor, but the sort
of pleasure which Shakspeare's plays give in the
acting seems to me not at all to differ from that
which the audience receive from those of other
writers ; and, *they being in themselves essentially
so different from all others*, I must conclude that
there is something in the nature of acting which
levels all distinctions. And, in fact, who does
not speak indifferently of the ' Gamester ' and of
'Macbeth' as fine stage performances, and praise
the Mrs. Beverley in the same way as the Lady
Macbeth of Mrs. S. ? Belvidera and Calista
and Isabella and Euphrasia, are they less liked
than Imogen, or than Juliet, or than Desdemona ? Are they not spoken of and remembered in the same way ? Is not the female
performer as great (as they call it) in one as in
the other ? Did not Garrick shine, and was he
not ambitious of shining, in every drawling

tragedy that his wretched day produced, — the
productions of the Hills and the Murphys and
the Browns, — and shall he have that honour to
dwell in our minds for ever as an inseparable
concomitant with Shakspeare ?　A kindred
mind !　Oh, who can read that affecting sonnet
of Shakspeare which alludes to his profession
as a player, —

> Oh, for my sake do you with Fortune chide,
> The guilty goddess of my harmful deeds,
> That did not better for my life provide
> Than public means which public manners breeds.
> Thence comes it that my name receives a brand,
> And almost thence my nature is subdued
> To what it works in, like the dyer's hand,—

Or that other confession, —

> Alas, 't is true, I have gone here and there,
> And made myself a motley to the view,
> Gored mine own thoughts, sold cheap what is most
> dear, —

Who can read these instances of jealous self-
watchfulness in our sweet Shakspeare and
dream of any congeniality between him and one
that, by every tradition of him, appears to have
been as mere a player as ever existed ; to have
had his mind tainted with the lowest player's
vices, — envy and jealousy and miserable crav-
ings after applause ; one who in the exercise of

his profession was jealous even of the women-
performers that stood in his way, — a manager
full of managerial tricks and stratagems and
finesse ; that any resemblance should be dreamed
of between him and Shakspeare, — Shakspeare,
who in the plenitude and consciousness of his
own powers could with that noble modesty
which we can neither imitate nor appreciate,
express himself thus of his own sense of his
own defects, —

> Wishing me like to one more rich in hope,
> Featured like him, like him with friends possessed :
> Desiring *this man's art, and that man's scope !*

I am almost disposed to deny to Garrick the
merits of being an admirer of Shakspeare. A
true lover of his excellences he certainly was
not ; for would any true lover of them have admitted into his matchless scenes such ribald trash
as Tate and Cibber and the rest of them, that

> With their darkness durst affront his light,

have foisted into the acting plays of Shakspeare ?
I believe it impossible that he could have had a
proper reverence for Shakspeare and have condescended to go through that interpolated scene
in ' Richard the Third ' in which Richard tries
to break his wife's heart by telling her he loves
another woman, and says, ' If she survives this

she is immortal.'   Yet I doubt not he delivered
this vulgar stuff with as much anxiety of em-
phasis as any of the genuine parts ; and for acting, it is as well calculated as any.   But we
have seen the part of Richard lately produce
great fame to an actor by his manner of playing
it, and it lets us into the secret of acting, and of
popular judgments of Shakspeare derived from
acting.   Not one of the spectators who have
witnessed Mr. C.'s exertions in that part but
has come away with a proper conviction that
Richard is a very wicked man, and kills little
children in their beds with something like the
pleasure which the giants and ogres in children's
books are represented to have taken in that
practice; moreover, that he is very close and
shrewd and devilish cunning, for you could see
that by his eye.

But is in fact this the impression we have in
reading the Richard of Shakspeare ?   Do we
feel anything like disgust, as we do at that
butcher-like representation of him that passes
for him on the stage ?   A horror at his crimes
blends with the effect which we feel ; but how
is it qualified, how is it carried off, by the rich
intellect which he displays, his resources, his
wit, his buoyant spirits, his vast knowledge and
insight into characters, the poetry of his part ! —

not an atom of all which is made perceivable in
Mr. C.'s way of acting it. Nothing but his
crimes, his actions, is visible, — they are promi-
nent and staring; the murderer stands out, — but
where is the lofty genius, the man of vast ca-
pacity, the profound, the witty, accomplished
Richard?

The truth is, the characters of Shakspeare are
so much the objects of meditation rather than of
interest or curiosity as to their actions that
while we are reading any of his great criminal
characters, — Macbeth, Richard, even Iago, —
we think not so much of the crimes which they
commit, as of the ambition, the aspiring spirit,
the intellectual activity which prompts them to
overleap those moral fences. Barnwell is a
wretched murderer; there is a certain fitness
between his neck and the rope ; he is the legitimate heir to the gallows ; nobody who thinks at
all can think of any alleviating circumstances in
his case to make him a fit object of mercy. Or
to take an instance from the higher tragedy,
what else but a mere assassin in Glenalvon ?
Do we think of anything but of the crime which
he commits and the rack which he deserves ?
That is all which we really think about him.
Whereas in corresponding characters in Shakspeare, so little do the actions comparatively

affect us, that while the impulses, the inner mind in all its perverted greatness, solely seems real, and is exclusively attended to, the crime is comparatively nothing. But when we see these things represented, the acts which they do are comparatively everything, their impulses nothing. The state of sublime emotion into which we are elevated by those images of night and horror which Macbeth is made to utter, that solemn prelude with which he entertains the time till the bell shall strike which is to call him to murder Duncan, — when we no longer read it in a book, when we have given up that vantage-ground of abstraction which reading possesses over seeing, and come to see a man in his bodily shape before our eyes actually preparing to commit a murder, if the acting be true and impressive, as I have witnessed it in Mr. K.'s performance of that part, the painful anxiety about the act, the natural longing to prevent it while it yet seems unperpetrated, the too close pressing semblance of reality, give a pain and an uneasiness which totally destroy all the delight which the words in the book convey, where the deed doing never presses upon us with the painful sense of presence ; it rather seems to belong to history, to something past and inevitable, if it has anything to do with time at all.

The sublime images, the poetry alone, is that which is present to our minds in the reading.

So to see Lear acted, — to see an old man tottering about the stage with a walking-stick, turned out of doors by his daughters in a rainy night, has nothing in it but what is painful and disgusting. We want to take him into shelter and relieve him, — that is all the feeling which the acting of Lear ever produced in me. But the Lear of Shakspeare cannot be acted. The contemptible machinery, by which they mimic the storm which he goes out in, is not more inadequate to represent the horrors of the real elements than any actor can be to represent Lear ; they might more easily propose to personate the Satan of Milton upon a stage, or one of Michael Angelo's terrible figures. The greatness of Lear is not in corporal dimension, but in intellectual ; the explosions of his passion are terrible as a volcano, — they are storms turning up and disclosing to the bottom that sea, his mind, with all its vast riches. It is his mind which is laid bare. This case of flesh and blood seems too insignificant to be thought on, even as he himself neglects it. On the stage we see nothing but corporal infirmities and weakness, the impotence of rage ; while we read it, we see not Lear, but we are Lear, — we are in his mind, we are sustained by a grandeur which baffles the malice of daughters and storms.   In the aberrations of his reason we discover a mighty, irregular power of reasoning, immethod- ized from the ordinary purposes of life, but ex- erting its powers, as the wind blows where it listeth, at will upon the corruptions and abuses of mankind.   What have looks or tones to do with that sublime identification of his age with that of the *heavens themselves*, when in his re- proaches to them for conniving at the injustice of his children he reminds them that ' they themselves are old ' ?   What gestures shall we appropriate to this ?   What has the voice or the eye to do with such things ?   But the play is beyond all art, as the tamperings with it show ; it is too hard and stony, — it must have love- scenes, and a happy ending.   It is not enough that Cordelia is a daughter, she must shine as a lover too.   Tate has put his hook in the nos- trils of this Leviathan, for Garrick and his fol- lowers, the showmen of scene, to draw the mighty beast about more easily.   A happy end- ing ! — as if the living martyrdom that Lear had gone through, the flaying of his feelings alive, did not make a fair dismissal from the stage of life the only decorous thing for him.   If he is to live and be happy after, if he could sustain this world's burden after, why all this pudder and preparation, why torment us with all this unnecessary sympathy ? As if the childish pleasure of getting his gilt robes and sceptre again could tempt him to act over again his misused station ; as if at his years, and with his experience, anything was left but to die !

' Lear ' is essentially impossible to be represented on a stage. But how many dramatic personages are there in Shakspeare which, though more tractable and feasible (if I may so speak) than Lear, yet from some circumstance, some adjunct to their character, are improper to be shown to our bodily eye. ' Othello,' for instance. Nothing can be more soothing, more flattering to the nobler parts of our natures, than to read of a young Venetian lady of highest extraction, through the force of love and from a sense of merit in him whom she loved, laying aside every consideration of kindred and country and colour, and wedding with a *coal-black Moor* (for such he is represented, in the imperfect state of knowledge respecting foreign countries in those days compared with our own, or in compliance with popular notions ; though the Moors are now well enough known to be by many shades less unworthy of white woman's fancy), — it is the perfect triumph of virtue over accidents, of the imagination over the senses. She sees Othello's colour in his mind. But upon the stage, when the imagination is no longer the ruling faculty, but we are left to our poor, unassisted senses, I appeal to every one that has seen 'Othello' played, whether he did not, on the contrary, sink Othello's mind in his colour; whether he did not find something extremely revolting in the courtship and wedded caresses of Othello and Desdemona; and whether the actual sight of the thing did not overweigh all that beautiful compromise which we make in reading. And the reason it should do so is obvious, because there is just so much reality presented to our senses as to give a per-ception of disagreement, with not enough of be-lief in the internal motives — all that which is unseen — to overpower and reconcile the first and obvious prejudices.[1] What we see upon a

---

[1] The error of supposing that because Othello's colour does not offend us in the reading, it should also not offend us in the seeing, is just such a fallacy as supposing that an Adam and Eve in a picture shall affect us just as they do in the poem. But in the poem we for a while have paradisaical senses given us, which vanish when we see a man and his wife without clothes in the picture. The painters themselves feel this, as is apparent by the awkward shifts they have recourse to, to make them look not quite naked, — by a sort of prophetic anachronism

stage is body and bodily action ; what we are conscious of in reading is almost exclusively the mind and its movements ; and this, I think, may sufficiently account for the very different sort of delight with which the same play so often affects us in the reading and the seeing.

It requires little reflection to perceive that if those characters in Shakspeare which are within the precincts of nature have yet something in them which appeals too exclusively to the imagination to admit of their being made objects to the senses without suffering a change and a diminution, — that still stronger the objection must lie against representing another line of characters which Shakspeare has introduced to give a wildness and a supernatural elevation to his scenes, as if to remove them still further from that assimilation to common life in which their excellence is vulgarly supposed to consist. When wc read the incantations of those terrible beings, the Witches in ' Macbeth,' though some of the ingredients of their hellish composition savour of the grotesque, yet is the effect upon us other than the most serious and appalling

antedating the invention of fig-leaves. So in the reading of the play, we see with Desdemona's eyes ; in the seeing of it, we are forced to look with our own.

that can be imagined ?   Do we not feel spell-
bound as Macbeth was ?   Can any mirth accompany a sense of their presence ?   We might
as well laugh under a consciousness of the principle of Evil himself being truly and really
present with us.   But attempt to bring these
beings on to a stage, and you turn them instantly
into so many old women that men and children
are to laugh at.   Contrary to the old saying,
that ' seeing is believing,' the sight actually
destroys the faith ; and the mirth in which we
indulge at their expense, when we see these
creatures upon a stage, seems to be a sort of
indemnification which we make to ourselves for
the terror which they put us in when reading
made them an object of belief, — when we sur-
rendered up our reason to the poet, as children
to their nurses and their elders ; and we laugh
at our fears, as children who thought they saw
something in the dark triumph when the bringing in of a candle discovers the vanity of their
fears.   For this exposure of supernatural agents
upon a stage is truly bringing in a candle to expose their own delusiveness.   It is the solitary
taper and the book that generates a faith in these
terrors ; a ghost by chandelier light and in
good company deceives no spectators, — a ghost
that can be measured by the eye, and his human

dimensions made out at leisure. The sight of a well-lighted house and a well-dressed audi-ence shall arm the most nervous child against any apprehensions, as Tom Brown says of the impenetrable skin of Achilles, with his impene-trable armour over it, ' Bully Dawson would have fought the devil with such advantages.'

Much has been said, and deservedly, in repro-bation of the vile mixture which Dryden has thrown into the ' Tempest ; ' doubtless without some such vicious alloy, the impure ears of that age would never have sat out to hear so much innocence of love as is contained in the sweet courtship of Ferdinand and Miranda. But is the ' Tempest ' of Shakspeare at all a subject for stage representation ? It is one thing to read of an enchanter, and to believe the wondrous tale while we are reading it ; but to have a conjuror brought before us in his conjuring-gown, with his spirits about him, which none but himself and some hundred of favoured spectators before the curtain are supposed to see, involves such a quantity of the *hateful incredible* that all our reverence for the author cannot hinder us from perceiving such gross attempts upon the senses to be in the highest degree childish and inef-ficient. Spirits and fairies cannot be repre-sented, they cannot even be painted ; they can

only be believed. But the elaborate and
anxious provision of scenery, which the luxury
of the age demands, in these cases works a quite
contrary effect to what is intended. That which
in comedy, or plays of familiar life, adds so
much to the life of the imitation, in plays which
appeal to the higher faculties positively destroys
the illusion which it is introduced to aid. A
parlour or a drawing-room, a library opening
into a garden, a garden with an alcove in it, a
street, or the piazza of Covent Garden, does
well enough in a scene ; we are content to give
as much credit to it as it demands ; or rather,
we think little about it, it is little more than
reading at the top of a page, ' Scene, a garden ; '
we do not imagine ourselves there, but we
readily admit the imitation of familiar objects.
But to think, by the help of painted trees and
caverns which we know to be painted, to trans-
port our minds to Prospero and his island and
his lonely cell,[1] or by the aid of a fiddle dex-
terously thrown in, in an interval of speaking,
to make us believe that we hear those super-

---

[1] It will be said these things are done in pictures.
But pictures and scenes are very different things. Paint-
ing is a word of itself; but in scene-painting there is the
attempt to deceive, and there is the discordancy, never to
be got over, between painted scenes and real people.

natural noises of which the isle was full, — the Orrery Lecturer at the Haymarket might as well hope, by his musical glasses cleverly stationed out of sight behind his apparatus, to make us believe that we do indeed hear the crystal spheres ring out that chime which, if it were to inwrap our fancy long, Milton thinks,

> Time would run back and fetch the age of gold,
> And speckled vanity
> Would sicken soon and die,
> And leprous Sin would melt from earthly mould, —
> Yea, Hell itself would pass away,
> And leave its dolorous mansions to the peering day.

The Garden of Eden, with our first parents in it, is not more impossible to be shown on a stage than the Enchanted Isle, with its no less interesting and innocent first settlers.

The subject of scenery is closely connected with that of the dresses, which are so anxiously attended to on our stage. I remember, the last time I saw Macbeth played, the discrepancy I felt at the changes of garment which he varied, — the shiftings and re-shiftings, like a Romish priest at mass. The luxury of stage-improvements and the importunity of the public eye require this. The coronation robe of the Scottish monarch was fairly a counterpart to that

N

which our king wears when he goes to the
parliament-house, — just so full and cumber-
some, and set out with ermine and pearls. And
if things must be represented, I see not what to
find fault with in this. But in reading, what
robe are we conscious of? Some dim images of
royalty, a crown and sceptre, may float before
our eyes, but who shall describe the fashion of
it? Do we see in our mind's eye what Webb
or any other robe-maker could pattern? This
is the inevitable consequence of imitating everything, to make all things natural. Whereas the
reading of a tragedy is a fine abstraction. It
presents to the fancy just so much of external
appearances as to make us feel that we are
among flesh and blood, while by far the greater
and better part of our imagination is employed
upon the thoughts and internal machinery of the
character. But in acting, scenery, dress, the
most contemptible things, call upon us to judge
of their naturalness.

Perhaps it would be no bad similitude to
liken the pleasure which we take in seeing one
of these fine plays acted, compared with that
quiet delight which we find in the reading of it,
to the different feelings with which a reviewer
and a man that is not a reviewer reads a
fine poem. The accursed critical habit, the

being called upon to judge and pronounce, must make it quite a different thing to the former. In seeing these plays acted, we are affected just as judges. When Hamlet compares the two pictures of Gertrude's first and second husband, who wants to see the pictures ? But in the acting, a miniature must be lugged out, — which we know not to be the picture, but only to show how finely a miniature may be represented. This showing of everything levels all things ; it makes tricks, bows, and courtesies of importance. Mrs. S. never got more fame by anything than by the manner in which she dismisses the guests in the banquet-scene in ' Macbeth ; ' it is as much remembered as any of her thrilling tones or impressive looks. But does such a trifle as this enter into the imaginations of the reader of that wild and wonderful scene ? Does not the mind dismiss the feasters as rapidly as it can ? Does it care about the gracefulness of the doing it ? But by acting, and judging of acting, all these non-essentials are raised into an importance injurious to the main interest of the play.

I have confined my observations to the tragic parts of Shakspeare. It would be no very difficult task to extend the inquiry to his comedies, and to show why Falstaff, Shallow, Sir Hugh

Evans, and the rest are equally incompatible with stage representation. The length to which this essay has run, will make it, I am afraid, sufficiently distasteful to the amateurs of the theatre, without going any deeper into the subject at present.

CHARACTERS OF DRAMATIC WRITERS CONTEMPORARY WITH SHAKSPEARE.

WHEN I selected for publication, in 1808, Specimens of English Dramatic Poets who lived about the time of Shakspeare, the kind of extracts which I was anxious to give were, not so much passages of wit and humor, though the old plays are rich in such, as scenes of passion, sometimes of the deepest quality, interesting situations, serious descriptions, that which is more nearly allied to poetry than to wit, and to tragic rather than to comic poetry. The plays which I made choice of were, with few exceptions, such as treat of human life and manners, rather than masques and Arcadian pastorals, with their train of abstractions, unimpassioned deities, passionate mortals, — Claius and Medorus and Amintas and Amarillis. My leading design was to illustrate what may be called the moral sense of our ancestors. To show in what manner they felt when they placed themselves by the power of imagination in trying circumstances, in the

conflicts of duty and passion, or the strife of
contending duties ; what sort of loves and en-
mities theirs were ; how their griefs were tempered, and their full-swoln joys abated ; how
much of Shakspeare shines in the great men his
contemporaries, and how far in his divine mind
and manners he surpassed them and all mankind.   I was also desirous to bring together some
of the most admired scenes of Fletcher and
Massinger, — in the estimation of the world the
only dramatic poets of that age entitled to be
considered after Shakspeare, — and by exhibiting
them in the same volume with the more impressive scenes of old Marlowe, Heywood, Tour-
neur, Webster, Ford, and others, to show what
we had slighted, while beyond all proportion
we had been crying up one or two favourite
names.   From the desultory criticisms which
accompanied that publication I have selected a
few which I thought would best stand by
themselves as requiring least immediate reference to the play or passage by which they
were suggested.

CHRISTOPHER MARLOWE.

Lust's Dominion, or the Lascivious Queen. —
This tragedy is in King Cambyses' vein, — rape

and murder and superlatives ; 'huffing braggart puft lines,' such as the play-writers anterior to Shakspeare are full of, and Pistol but coldly imitates.

Tamburlaine the Great, or the Scythian Shepherd. — The lunes of Tamburlaine are perfect midsummer madness. Nebuchadnezzar's are mere modest pretensions compared with the thundering vaunts of this Scythian Shepherd. He comes in, drawn by conquered kings, and reproaches these *pampered jades of Asia* that they can *draw but twenty miles a day*. Till I saw this passage with my own eyes I never believed that it was anything more than a pleasant burlesque of mine ancient's. But I can assure my readers that it is soberly set down in a play which their ancestors took to be serious.

Edward the Second. — In a very different style from mighty ' Tamburlaine ' is the tragedy of ' Edward the Second.' The reluctant pangs of abdicating royalty in Edward furnished hints which Shakspeare scarcely improved in his ' Richard the Second ; ' and the death-scene of Marlowe's king moves pity and terror beyond any scene, ancient or modern, with which I am acquainted.

The Rich Jew of Malta. — Marlowe's Jew does not approach so near to Shakspeare's as his ' Edward the Second' does to ' Richard the Second.'   Barabas is a mere monster brought in with a large painted nose to please the rabble. He kills in sport, poisons whole nunneries, invents infernal machines.   He is just such an exhibition as a century or two earlier might have been played before the Londoners ' by the royal command,' when a general pillage and massacre of the Hebrews had been previously resolved on in the cabinet.   It is curious to see a superstition wearing out.   The idea of a Jew, which our pious ancestors contemplated with so much horror, has nothing in it now revolting.   We have tamed the claws of the beast, and pared its nails, and now we take it to our arms, fondle it, write plays to flatter it ; it is visited by princes, affects a taste, patronizes the arts, and is the only liberal and gentlemanlike thing in Christendom.

Doctor Faustus. — The growing horrors of Faustus's last scene are awfully marked by the hours and half-hours as they expire, and bring him nearer and nearer to the exactment of his dire compact.   It is indeed an agony and a fearful colluctation.   Marlowe is said to have been tainted with atheistical positions, to have denied God and the Trinity.   To such a genius the history of Faustus must have been delectable food : to wander in fields where curiosity is forbidden to go, to approach the dark gulf near enough to look in, to be busied in speculations which are the rottenest part of the core of the fruit that fell from the tree of knowledge.[1] Barabas the Jew and Faustus the conjuror are offsprings of a mind which at least delighted to dally with interdicted subjects. They both talk a language which a believer would have been tender of putting into the mouth of a character though but in fiction. But the holiest minds have sometimes not thought it reprehensible to counterfeit impiety in the person of another, to bring Vice upon the stage speaking her own dialect ; and, themselves being armed with an unction of self-confident impunity, have not scrupled to handle and touch that familiarly which would be death to others. Milton in the person of Satan has started speculations hardier than any which the feeble armoury of the atheist ever furnished ; and the precise, strait-laced Richardson has strengthened Vice, from the mouth of Lovelace, with entangling sophistries and abstruse pleas against her adversary,

---

[1] Error, entering into the world with Sin among us poor Adamites, may be said to spring from the tree of knowledge itself and from the rotten kernels of that fatal apple. — *Howell's Letters.*

Virtue, which Sedley, Villiers, and Rochester wanted depth of libertinism enough to have invented.

THOMAS DECKER.

Old Fortunatus. — The humour of a frantic lover, in the scene where Orleans to his friend Galloway defends the passion with which himself, being a prisoner in the English king's court, is enamoured to frenzy of the king's daughter Agripyna, is done to the life. Orleans is as passionate an inamorata as any which Shakspeare ever drew. He is just such another adept in Love's reasons. The sober people of the world are with him —

A swarm of fools
Crowding together to be counted wise.

He talks ' pure Biron and Romeo,' he is almost as poetical as they, quite as philosophical, only a little madder. After all, Love's sectaries are a reason unto themselves. We have gone retrograde to the noble heresy since the days when Sidney proselyted our nation to this mixed health and disease ; the kindliest symptom, yet the most alarming crisis in the ticklish state of youth ; the nourisher and the destroyer of hopeful wits ; the mother of twin births, wisdom and folly, valour and weakness ; the servitude above freedom ; the gentle mind's religion ; the liberal superstition.

The Honest Whore. — There is in the second part of this play, where Bellafront, a reclaimed harlot, recounts some of the miseries of her profession, a simple picture of honour and shame, contrasted without violence, and expressed without immodesty, which is worth all the *strong lines* against the harlot's profession with which both parts of this play are offensively crowded. A satirist is always to be suspected who, to make vice odious, dwells upon all its acts and minutest circumstances with a sort of relish and retrospective fondness. But so near are the boundaries of panegyric and invective that a worn-out sinner is sometimes found to make the best declaimer against sin. The same high-seasoned descriptions, which in his unregenerate state served but to inflame his appetites, in his new province of a moralist will serve him, a little turned, to expose the enormity of those appetites in other men. When Cervantes with such proficiency of fondness dwells upon the Don's library, who sees not that he has been a great reader of books of knight-errantry, — perhaps was at some time of his life in danger of falling into those very extravagances which he ridiculed so happily in his hero ?

JOHN MARSTON.

Antonio and Mellida. — The situation of An-drugio and Lucio in the first part of this tragedy — where Andrugio, Duke of Genoa, banished his country, with the loss of a son supposed drowned, is cast upon the territory of his mortal enemy, the Duke of Venice, with no attendants but Lucio, an old nobleman, and a page — resembles that of Lear and Kent in that king's distresses. Andrugio, like Lear, mani-fests a kinglike impatience, a turbulent great-ness, an affected resignation. The enemies which he enters lists to combat, ' Despair and mighty Grief and sharp Impatience,' and the forces which he brings to vanquish them, ' cor-nets of horse,' etc., are in the boldest style of allegory. They are such a ' race of mourners ' as the ' infection of sorrows loud ' in the intel-lect might beget on some ' pregnant cloud ' in the imagination. The prologue to the second part, for its passionate earnestness and for the tragic note of preparation which it sounds, might have preceded one of those old tales of

' Thebes or Pelops' line ' which Milton has so highly commended as free from the common error of the poets in his day of ' intermixing comic stuff with tragic sadness and gravity, brought in without discretion corruptly to gratify the people.' It is as solemn a preparative as the ' warning voice which he who saw the Apocalypse heard cry.'

What You Will.—O, I shall ne'er forget how he went cloath'd. Act I. Scene 1. — To judge of the liberality of these notions of dress, we must advert to the days of Gresham, and the consternation which a phenomenon habited like the merchant here described would have excited among the flat round caps and cloth stockings upon 'Change when those ' original arguments or tokens of a citizen's vocation were in fashion, not more for thrift and usefulness than for distinction and grace.' The blank uniformity to which all professional distinctions in apparel have been long hastening, is one instance of the decay of symbols among us, which, whether it has contributed or not to make us a more intellectual, has certainly made us a less imaginative, people. Shakspeare knew the force of signs : a ' malignant and a turban'd Turk.' This ' meal-cap miller,' says the author of ' God's Revenge against Murder,' to express

his indignation at an atrocious outrage committed by the miller Pierot upon the person
of the fair Marieta.

AUTHOR UNKNOWN.

The Merry Devil of Edmonton. — The scene
in this delightful comedy, in which Jerningham,
'with the true feeling of a zealous friend,'
touches the griefs of Mounchensey, seems
written to make the reader happy.   Few of our
dramatists or novelists have attended enough to
this.   They torture and wound us abundantly.
They are economists only in delight.   Nothing
can be finer, more gentlemanlike, and nobler
than the conversation and compliments of these
young men.   How delicious is Raymond Mounchensey's forgetting, in his fears, that Jerningham has a ' Saint in Essex,' and how sweetly
his friend reminds him !   I wish it could be as-
certained, which there is some grounds for believing, that Michael Drayton was the author of
this piece.   It would add a worthy appendage
to the renown of that panegyrist of my native
earth, who has gone over her soil, in his ' Poly-
olbion,' with the fidelity of a herald and the
painful love of a son ; who has not left a rivulet,
so narrow that it may be stept over, without

honourable mention ; and has animated hills and streams with life and passion beyond the dreams of old mythology.

THOMAS HEYWOOD.

A Woman Killed with Kindness. — Heywood is a sort of *prose* Shakspeare ; his scenes are to the full as natural and affecting. But we miss *the poet,* that which in Shakspeare always appears out and above the surface of *the nature.* Heywood's characters in this play, for instance, his country gentlemen, etc., are exactly what we see, but of the best kind of what we see in life. Shakspeare makes us believe, while we are among his lovely creations, that they are nothing but what we are familiar with, as in dreams new things seem old ; but we awake, and sigh for the difference.

The English Traveller. — Heywood's preface to this play is interesting, as it shows the heroic indifference about the opinion of posterity, which some of these great writers seem to have felt. There is a magnanimity in authorship as in everything else. His ambition seems to have been confined to the pleasure of hearing the players speak his lines while he lived. It does not appear that he ever contemplated the

possibility of being read by after ages. What a
slender pittance of fame was motive sufficient to
the production of such plays as the 'English
Traveller,' the 'Challenge for Beauty,' and the
'Woman Killed with Kindness.' Posterity is
bound to take care that a writer loses nothing
by such a noble modesty.

THOMAS MIDDLETON AND WILLIAM ROWLEY.

A Fair Quarrel. — The insipid levelling morality to which the modern stage is tied down,
would not admit of such admirable passions
as these scenes are filled with.   A puritanical
obtuseness of sentiment, a stupid infantile
goodness, is creeping among us, instead of
the vigorous passions, and virtues clad in
flesh and blood, with which the old dramatists
present us.   Those noble and liberal casuists
could discern in the differences, the quarrels,
the animosities of men, a beauty and truth
of moral feeling, no less than in the everlast-
ingly inculcated duties of forgiveness and
atonement.   With us, all is hypocritical meek-
ness.   A reconciliation-scene, be the occasion
never so absurd, never fails of applause.   Our
audiences come to the theatre to be compli-

mented on their goodness. They compare notes
with the amiable characters in the play, and find
a wonderful sympathy of disposition between
them. We have a common stock of dramatic
morality, out of which a writer may be supplied
without the trouble of copying it from originals
within his own breast. To know the boundaries of honour, to be judiciously valiant, to have
a temperance which shall beget a smoothness in
the angry swellings of youth, to esteem life as
nothing when the sacred reputation of a parent
is to be defended, yet to shake and tremble
under a pious cowardice when that ark of an
honest confidence.is found to be frail and tottering, to feel the true blows of a real disgrace
blunting that sword which the imaginary strokes
of a supposed false imputation had put so keen
an edge upon but lately, — to do, or to imagine
this done in a feigned story, asks something
more of a moral sense, somewhat a greater delicacy of perception in questions of right and
wrong, than goes to the writing of two or
three hackneyed sentences about the laws of
honour, as opposed to the laws of the land, or a
commonplace against duelling. Yet such things
would stand a writer nowadays in far better
stead than Captain Agar and his conscientious
honour; and he would be considered as a far

better teacher of morality than old Rowley or
Middleton, if they were living.

WILLIAM ROWLEY.

A New Wonder; a Woman Never Vext. —
The old play-writers are distinguished by an
honest boldness of exhibition; they show everything without being ashamed. If a reverse in
fortune is to be exhibited, they fairly bring us
to the prison-grate and the alms-basket. A
poor man on our stage is always a gentleman;
he may be known by a peculiar neatness of
apparel, and by wearing black. Our delicacy,
in fact, forbids the dramatizing of distress at all.
It is never shown in its essential properties; it
appears but as the adjunct of some virtue, as
something which is to be relieved, from the
approbation of which relief the spectators are to
derive a certain soothing of self-referred satisfaction. We turn away from the real es-
sences of things to hunt after their relative
shadows, — moral duties; whereas, if the truth
of things were fairly represented, the relative
duties might be safely trusted to themselves,
and moral philosophy lose the name of a
science.

THOMAS MIDDLETON.

The Witch. — Though some resemblance may
be traced between the charms in 'Macbeth' and
the incantations in this play, which is supposed
to have preceded it, this coincidence will not
detract much from the originality of Shakspeare.
His witches are distinguished from the witches
of Middleton by essential differences. These
are creatures to whom man or woman, plotting
some dire mischief, might resort for occasional
consultation. Those originate deeds of blood,
and begin bad impulses to men. From the
moment that their eyes first meet with Macbeth's, he is spell-bound. That meeting sways
his destiny. He can never break the fascina-
tion. These witches can hurt the body, those
have power over the soul. Hecate in Middleton has a son, a low buffoon ; the hags of Shakspeare have neither child of their own, nor
seem to be descended from any parent. They
are foul anomalies, of whom we know not
whence they are sprung, nor whether they have
beginning or ending. As they are without
human passions, so they seem to be without
human relations. They come with thunder and
lightning, and vanish to airy music. This is all

we know of them. Except Hecate, they have
no *names*, — which heightens their mysterious-
ness. The names, and some of the properties,
which the other author has given to his hags
excite smiles. The Weird Sisters are serious
things ; their presence cannot co-exist with
mirth. But, in a lesser degree, the witches of
Middleton are fine creations. Their power,
too, is in some measure over the mind. They
raise jars, jealousies, strifes, 'like a thick scurf,'
over life.

WILLIAM ROWLEY, THOMAS DECKER,
JOHN FORD, ETC.

The Witch of Edmonton. — Mother Sawyer,
in this wild play, differs from the hags of both
Middleton and Shakspeare. She is the plain,
traditional old woman witch of our ancestors, —
poor, deformed, and ignorant ; the terror of
villages, herself amenable to a justice. That
should be a hardy sheriff, with the power of
the county at his heels, that would lay hands
upon the Weird Sisters. They are of another
jurisdiction. But upon the common and received opinion, the author (or authors) have

engrafted strong fancy. There is something frightfully earnest in her invocations to the Familiar.

CYRIL TOURNEUR.

The Revengers' Tragedy. — The reality and life of the dialogue in which Vindici and Hippolito first tempt their mother, and then threaten her with death for consenting to the dishonour of their sister, passes any scenical illusion I ever felt. I never read it but my ears tingle and I feel a hot blush overspread my cheeks, as if I were presently about to proclaim such malefactions of myself as the brothers here rebuke in their unnatural parent, in words more keen and dagger-like than those which Hamlet speaks to his mother. Such power has the passion of shame truly personated, not only to strike guilty creatures unto the soul, but to 'appal' even those that are 'free.'

JOHN WEBSTER.

The Duchess of Malfy. — All the several parts of the dreadful apparatus with which the death of the Duchess is ushered in, — the waxen images which counterfeit death, the wild masque

of madmen, the tomb-maker, the bellman, the
living person's dirge, the mortification by degrees, — are not more remote from the conceptions of ordinary vengeance than the strange
character of suffering which they seem to bring
upon their victim is out of the imagination of
ordinary poets.   As they are not like inflictions
of this life, so her language seems not of this
world.   She has lived among horrors till she
is become 'native and endowed unto that element.'   She speaks the dialect of despair ; her
tongue has a smatch of Tartarus and the souls
in bale.   To move a horror skilfully, to touch a
soul to the quick, to lay upon fear as much as
it can bear, to wean and weary a life till it is
ready to drop, and then step in with mortal
instruments to take its last forfeit, — this only a
Webster can do.   Inferior geniuses may ' upon
horror's head horrors accumulate,' but they
cannot do this.   They mistake quantity for
quality ; they 'terrify babes with painted devils,'
but they know not how a soul is to be moved.
Their terrors want dignity, their affrightments
are without decorum.

The White Devil, or Vittoria Corombona. —
This White Devil of Italy sets off a bad cause
so speciously, and pleads with such an inno-
cence-resembling boldness, that we seem to see

that matchless beauty of her face which inspires such gay confidence into her, and are ready to expect, when she has done her pleadings, that her very judges, her accusers, the grave ambassadors who sit as spectators, and all the court, will rise and make proffer to defend her in spite of the utmost conviction of her guilt, — as the Shepherds in ' Don Quixote' make proffer to follow the beautiful Shepherdess Marcela, ' without making any profit of her manifest resolution made there in their hearing.'

> So sweet and lovely does she make the shame,
> Which, like a canker in the fragrant rose,
> Does spot the beauty of her budding name !

I never saw anything like the funeral dirge in this play, for the death of Marcello, except the ditty which reminds Ferdinand of his drowned father in the ' Tempest.' As that is of the water, watery, so this is of the earth, earthy. Both have that intenseness of feeling which seems to resolve itself into the element which it contemplates.

In a note on the ' Spanish Tragedy ' in the Specimens, I have said that there is nothing in the undoubted plays of Jonson which would authorize us to suppose that he could have supplied the additions to 'Hieronymo.' I suspected the agency of some more potent spirit. I thought that Webster might have furnished them. They seemed full of that wild, solemn, preternatural cast of grief which bewilders us in the Duchess of Malfy. On second considera- tion, I think this a hasty criticism. They are more like the overflowing griefs and talking distraction of Titus Andronicus. The sorrows of the Duchess set inward ; if she talks, it is little more than soliloquy imitating conversation in a kind of bravery.

JOHN FORD.

The Broken Heart. — I do not know where to find, in any play, a catastrophe so grand, so solemn, and so surprising as in this. This is indeed, according to Milton, to describe high passions and high actions. The fortitude of the Spartan boy who let a beast gnaw out his bowels till he died, without expressing a groan, is a faint bodily image of this dilaceration of the spirit, and exenteration of the inmost mind, which Calantha, with a holy violence against her nature, keeps closely covered till the last duties of a wife and a queen are fulfilled. Stories of martyrdom are but of chains and the stake, — a little bodily suffering. These torments—

> On the purest spirits prey,
> As on entrails, joints, and limbs,
> With answerable pains, but more intense.

What a noble thing is the soul in its strengths and in its weaknesses! Who would be less weak than Calantha? Who can be so strong? The expression of this transcendent scene almost bears us in imagination to Calvary and the Cross; and we seem to perceive some analogy between the scenical sufferings which we are here contemplating, and the real agonies of that final completion to which we dare no more than hint a reference. Ford was of the first order of poets. He sought for sublimity, not by parcels, in metaphors or visible images, but directly where she has her full residence in the heart of man, — in the actions and sufferings of the greatest minds. There is a grandeur of the soul above mountains, seas, and the elements. Even in the poor perverted reason of Giovanni and Annabella, in the play[1] which stands at the head of the modern collection of the works of this author, we discern traces of that fiery particle which, in the irregular

[1] 'Tis pity she is a Whore.

starting from out the road of beaten action, discovers something of a right line even in obliquity, and shows hints of an improvable greatness in the lowest descents and degradations of our nature.

FULKE GREVILLE, LORD BROOKE.

Alaham, Mustapha. — The two tragedies of Lord Brooke, printed among his poems, might with more propriety have been termed political treatises than plays. Their author has strangely contrived to make passion, character, and interest, of the highest order, subservient to the expression of state dogmas and mysteries. He is nine parts Machiavel and Tacitus, for one part Sophocles or Seneca. In this writer's estimate of the powers of the mind, the understanding must have held a most tyrannical preeminence. Whether we look into his plays or his most passionate love-poems, we shall find all frozen and made rigid with intellect. The finest movements of the human heart, the utmost grandeur of which the soul is capable, are essentially comprised in the actions and speeches of Cælica and Camena. Shakspeare, who seems to have had a peculiar delight in contemplating womanly perfection, whom for his many sweet images of female excellence all women are in an especial manner bound to love, has not raised the ideal of the female character higher than Lord Brooke, in these two women, has done. But it requires a study equivalent to the learning of a new language to understand their meaning when they speak. It is indeed hard to hit, —

> Much like thy riddle, Samson, in one day
> Or seven, though one should musing sit.

It is as if a being of pure intellect should take upon him to express the emotions of our sensitive natures. There would be all knowledge, but sympathetic expressions would be wanting.

BEN JONSON.

The Case is Altered. — The passion for wealth has worn out much of its grossness in tract of time. Our ancestors certainly conceived of money as able to confer a distinct gratification in itself, not considered simply as a symbol of wealth. The old poets, when they introduce a miser, make him address his gold as his mistress ; as something to be seen, felt, and

hugged ; as capable of satisfying two of the
senses at least.   The substitution of a thin,
unsatisfying medium in the place of the good
old tangible metal has made avarice quite a
Platonic affection in comparison with the seeing, touching, and handling pleasures of the
old Chrysophilites.   A bank-note can no more
satisfy the touch of a true sensualist in this
passion than Creusa could return her husband's
embrace in the shades.   See the Cave of Mammon in Spenser ; Barabas' contemplation of his
wealth in the ' Rich Jew of Malta ; ' Luke's rap-
tures in the 'City Madam ;' the idolatry and absolute gold-worship of the miser Jaques in this early
comic production of Ben Jonson's.   Above all,
hear Guzman, in that excellent old translation
of the ' Spanish Rogue,' expatiate on the ' ruddy
cheeks of your golden ruddocks, your Spanish
pistolets, your plump and full-faced Portuguese,
and your clear-skinned pieces of eight of Cas-
tile,' which he and his fellows the beggars kept
secret to themselves, and did privately enjoy in
a plentiful manner.   ' For to have them, to pay
them away, is not to enjoy them ; to enjoy
them is to have them lying by us, having no
other need of them than to use them for the
clearing of the eye-sight and the comforting of
our senses.   These we did carry about with us,

sewing them in some patches of our doublets near unto the heart, and as close to the skin as we could handsomely quilt them in, holding them to be restorative.'

Poetaster. — This Roman play seems written to confute those enemies of Ben in his own days and ours who have said that he made a pedantical use of his learning. He has here revived the whole court of Augustus by a learned spell. We are admitted to the society of the illustrious dead. Virgil, Horace, Ovid, Tibullus, converse in our own tongue more finely and poetically than they were used to express themselves in their native Latin. Nothing can be imagined more elegant, refined, and court-like than the scenes between this Louis the Fourteenth of antiquity and his literati. The whole essence and secret of that kind of intercourse is contained therein. The economical liberality by which greatness, seeming to waive some part of its prerogative, takes care to lose none of the essentials ; the prudential liberties of an inferior, which flatter by commanded boldness and soothe with complimentary sincerity. These, and a thousand beautiful passages from his ' New Inn,' his 'Cynthia's Revels,' and from those numerous court-masques and entertainments which he was in the daily habit of

furnishing, might be adduced to show the poetical fancy and elegance of mind of the supposed
rugged old bard.

Alchemist. — The judgment is perfectly over-
whelmed by the torrent of images, words, and
book-knowledge with which Epicure Mammon
(Act II. Scene 2) confounds and stuns his in-
credulous hearer. They come pouring out like
the successive falls of Nilus. They 'doubly
redouble strokes upon the foe.' Description
outstrides proof. We are made to believe
effects before we have testimony for their
causes. If there is no one image which attains
the height of the sublime, yet the confluence
and assemblage of them all produces a result
equal to the grandest poetry. The huge Xer-
xean army countervails against single Achilles.
Epicure Mammon is the most determined off-
spring of its author. It has the whole 'matter
and copy of the father, — eye, nose, lip, the
trick of his frown.' It is just such a swaggerer
as contemporaries have described old Ben to
be. Meercraft, Bobadil, the Host of the New
Inn, have all his image and superscription.
But Mammon is arrogant pretension personi-
fied. Sir Samson Legend, in 'Love for Love,'
is such another lying, overbearing character,
but he does not come up to Epicure Mammon.

What a ' towering bravery' there is in his sen-
suality ! he affects no pleasure under a Sultan.
It is as if 'Egypt with Assyria strove in
luxury.'

GEORGE CHAPMAN.

*Bussy D'Ambois, Byron's Conspiracy, Byron's
Tragedy*, *etc.* — Webster has happily character-
ized the 'full and heightened style' of Chapman, who of all the English play-writers
perhaps approaches nearest to Shakspeare in
the descriptive and didactic, in passages which
are less purely dramatic. He could not go
out of himself, as Shakspeare could shift at
pleasure, to inform and animate other existences,
but in himself he had an eye to perceive and a
soul to embrace all forms and modes of being.
He would have made a great epic poet, if indeed he has not abundantly shown himself to be
one ; for his Homer is not so properly a translation as the stories of Achilles and Ulysses re-
written. The earnestness and passion which he
has put into every part of these poems would be
incredible to a reader of mere modern translations. His almost Greek zeal for the glory of
his heroes can only be paralleled by that fierce

spirit of Hebrew bigotry with which Milton, as
if personating one of the zealots of the old law,
clothed himself when he sat down to paint the
acts of Samson against the uncircumcised. The
great obstacle to Chapman's translations being
read, is their unconquerable quaintness. He
pours out in the same breath the most just and
natural, and the most violent and crude expressions. He seems to grasp at whatever words
come first to hand while the enthusiasm is upon
him, as if all other must be inadequate to the
divine meaning. But passion (the all-in-all in
poetry) is everywhere present, raising the low,
dignifying the mean, and putting sense into the
absurd. He makes his readers glow, weep,
tremble, take any affection which he pleases, be
moved by words, or, in spite of them, be dis-
gusted and overcome their disgust.

Francis Beaumont. — John Fletcher.

Maid's Tragedy. — One characteristic of the
excellent old poets is, their being able to bestow
grace upon subjects which naturally do not seem
susceptible of any. I will mention two instances.
Zelmane in the 'Arcadia' of Sidney, and Helena
in the 'All 's Well that Ends Well' of Shakspeare.

What can be more unpromising at first sight
than the idea of a young man disguising himself
in woman's attire, and passing himself off for a
woman among women ; and that for a long
space of time? Yet Sir Philip has preserved so
matchless a decorum that neither does Pyrocles'
manhood suffer any stain for the effeminacy of
Zelmane, nor is the respect due to the princesses
at all diminished when the deception comes to
be known. In the sweetly constituted mind of
Sir Philip Sidney it seems as if no ugly thought
or unhandsome meditation could find a harbour.
He turned all that he touched into images of
honour and virtue. Helena in Shakspeare is a
young woman seeking a man in marriage. The
ordinary rules of courtship are reversed, the
habitual feelings are crossed. Yet with such
exquisite address this dangerous subject is
handled that Helena's forwardness loses her no
honour ; delicacy dispenses with its laws in her
favour, and nature, in her single case, seems
content to suffer a sweet violation. Aspatia, in
the ' Maid's Tragedy,' is a character equally difficult, with Helena, of being managed with grace.
She too is a slighted woman, refused by the
man who had once engaged to marry her. Yet
it is artfully contrived that while we pity we
respect her, and she descends without degrada-

P

tion. Such wonders true poetry and passion can do, to confer dignity upon subjects which do not seem capable of it. But Aspatia must not be compared at all points with Helena ; she does not so absolutely predominate over her situation, but she suffers some diminution, some abatement of the full lustre of the female character, which Helena never does. Her character has many degrees of sweetness, some of delicacy ; but it has weakness, which, if we do not despise, we are sorry for. After all, Beaumont and Fletcher were but an inferior sort of Shakspeares and Sidneys.

Philaster. — The character of Bellario must have been extremely popular in its day. For many years after the date of 'Philaster's' first exhibition on the stage, scarce a play can be found without one of these women pages in it, following in the train of some pre-engaged lover, calling on the gods to bless her happy rival (his mistress), whom no doubt she secretly curses in her heart, giving rise to many pretty *équivoques* by the way on the confusion of sex, and either made happy at last by some surprising turn of fate, or dismissed with the joint pity of the lovers and the audience. Donne has a copy of verses to his mistress dissuading her from a resolution, which she seems to have

taken up from some of these scenical represen-
tations, of following him abroad as a page. It
is so earnest, so weighty, so rich in poetry, in
sense, in wit and pathos, that it deserves to
be read as a solemn close in future to all such
sickly fancies as he there deprecates.

JOHN FLETCHER.

Thierry and Theodoret. — The scene where
Ordella offers her life a sacrifice, that the king
of France may not be childless, I have always
considered as the finest in all Fletcher, and
Ordella to be the most perfect notion of the
female heroic character, next to Calantha in the
'Broken Heart.' She is a piece of sainted nature.
Yet noble as the whole passage is, it must be
confessed that the manner of it, compared with
Shakspeare's finest scenes, is faint and languid.
Its motion is circular, not progressive. Each
line revolves on itself in a sort of separate orbit ;
they do not join into one another like a run-
ning-hand. Fletcher's ideas moved slow ; his
versification, though sweet, is tedious, — it stops
at every turn ; he lays line upon line, making
up one after the other, adding image to image
so deliberately that we see their junctures.

Shakspeare mingles everything, runs line into line, embarrasses sentences and metaphors ; before one idea has burst its shell, another is hatched and clamorous for disclosure. Another striking difference between Fletcher and Shakspeare is the fondness of the former for unnatural and violent situations. He seems to have thought that nothing great could be produced in an ordinary way. The chief incidents in some of his most admired tragedies show this.[1] Shakspeare had nothing of this contortion in his mind, none of that craving after violent situations, and flights of strained and improbable virtue, which I think always betrays an imperfect moral sensibility. The wit of Fletcher is excellent,[2] like his serious scenes, but there is something strained and far-fetched in both. He is too mistrustful of Nature ; he always goes a little on one side of her. Shakspeare chose her without a reserve ; and had riches, power, understanding, and length of days, with her, for a dowry.

Faithful Shepherdess. — If all the parts of this delightful pastoral had been in unison with its many innocent scenes and sweet lyric inter-

---

[1] Wife for a Month, Cupid's Revenge, Double Marriage, etc.

[2] Wit without Money, and his comedies generally.

mixtures, it had been a poem fit to vie with 'Comus' or the 'Arcadia,' to have been put into the hands of boys and virgins, to have made matter for young dreams, like the loves of Hermia and Lysander. But a spot is on the face of this Diana. Nothing short of infatuation could have driven Fletcher upon mixing with this 'blessedness' such an ugly deformity as Cloe, the wanton shepherdess! If Cloe was meant to set off Clorin by contrast, Fletcher should have known that such weeds by juxtaposition do not set off, but kill sweet flowers.

PHILIP MASSINGER. — THOMAS DECKER.

The Virgin Martyr. — This play has some beauties of so very high an order that with all my respect for Massinger I do not think he had poetical enthusiasm capable of rising up to them. His associate, Decker, who wrote ' Old Fortunatus,' had poetry enough for anything. The very impurities which obtrude themselves among the sweet pieties of this play, like Satan among the Sons of Heaven, have a strength of contrast, a raciness, and a glow, in them, which are beyond Massinger. They are to the religion of the rest what Caliban is to Miranda.

PHILIP MASSINGER. — THOMAS MIDDLETON. —
WILLIAM ROWLEY.

Old Law. — There is an exquisiteness of
moral sensibility, making one's eyes to gush out
tears of delight, and a poetical strangeness in
the circumstances of this sweet tragi-comedy,
which are unlike anything in the dramas which
Massinger wrote alone. The pathos is of a
subtler edge. Middleton and Rowley, who
assisted in it, had both of them finer geniuses
than their associate.

JAMES SHIRLEY

Claims a place amongst the worthies of this
period, not so much for any transcendent talent
in himself, as that he was the last of a great
race, all of whom spoke nearly the same language and had a set of moral feelings and
notions in common. A new language, and
quite a new turn of tragic and comic interest,
came in with the Restoration.

BARBARA S——.

ON the noon of the 14th of November, 1743 or 1744, I forget which it was, just as the clock had struck one, Barbara S ——, with her accustomed punctuality, ascended the long, rambling staircase, with awkward, interposed landing-places, which led to the office, or rather a sort of box with a desk in it, whereat sat the then treasurer of (what few of our readers may remember) the old Bath Theatre. All over the island it was the custom, and remains so, I believe, to this day, for the players to receive their weekly stipend on the Saturday. It was not much that Barbara had to claim.

The little maid had just entered her eleventh year; but her important station at the theatre, as it seemed to her, with the benefits which she felt to accrue from her pious application of her small earnings, had given an air of womanhood to her steps and to her behaviour. You would have taken her to have been at least five years older.

Till latterly she had merely been employed in choruses, or where children were wanted to fill up the scene.   But the manager, observing a diligence and adroitness in her above her age, had for some few months past intrusted to her the performance of whole parts.   You may guess the self-consequence of the promoted Barbara.   She had already drawn tears in young Arthur ; had rallied Richard with infantine petulance in the Duke of York ; and in her turn had rebuked that petulance when she was Prince of Wales.   She would have done the elder child in Morton's pathetic afterpiece to the life ; but as yet the 'Children in the Wood' was not.

Long after this little girl was grown an aged woman, I have seen some of these small parts, each making two or three pages at most, copied out in the rudest hand of the then prompter, who doubtless transcribed a little more carefully and fairly for the grown-up tragedy ladies of the establishment.   But such as they were, blotted and scrawled, as for a child's use, she kept them all ; and in the zenith of her after reputation it was a delightful sight to behold them bound up in costliest morocco, each single, each small part making a *book*, with fine clasps, gilt-splashed, etc.   She had conscientiously kept them as they had been delivered to her; not a blot had been effaced or tampered with. They were precious to her for their affecting remembrancings. They were her principia, her rudiments; the elementary atoms, the little steps by which she pressed forward to perfection. 'What,' she would say, 'could India-rubber, or a pumice-stone, have done for these darlings?'

I am in no hurry to begin my story, — indeed I have little or none to tell, — so I will just mention an observation of hers connected with that interesting time.

Not long before she died I had been discoursing with her on the quantity of real present emotion which a great tragic performer experiences during acting. I ventured to think that though in the first instance such players must have possessed the feelings which they so powerfully called up in others, yet by frequent repetition those feelings must become deadened in great measure, and the performer trust to the memory of past emotion, rather than express a present one. She indignantly repelled the notion that with a truly great tragedian the operation by which such effects were produced upon an audience could ever degrade itself into what was purely mechanical. With much delicacy, avoiding to instance in her *self*-experience, she told me that so long ago as when she used to play the part of the Little Son to Mrs. Porter's Isabella (I think it was), when that impressive actress has been bending over her in some heartrending colloquy, she has felt real hot tears come trickling from her, which (to use her powerful expression) have perfectly scalded her back.

I am not quite so sure that it was Mrs. Porter, but it was some great actress of that day. The name is indifferent; but the fact of the scalding tears I most distinctly remember.

I was always fond of the society of players, and am not sure that an impediment in my speech (which certainly kept me out of the pulpit), even more than certain personal disqualifications, which are often got over in that profession, did not prevent me at one time of life from adopting it. I have had the honour (I must ever call it) once to have been admitted to the tea-table of Miss Kelly. I have played at serious whist with Mr. Liston. I have chatted with ever good-humoured Mrs. Charles Kemble. I have conversed as friend to friend with her accomplished husband. I have been indulged with a classical conference with Macready, and with a sight of the Player-picture gallery, at Mr. Mathews's when the kind owner, to remunerate me for my love of the old actors (whom he loves so much), went over it with me, supplying to his capital collection what alone the artist could not give them, — voice, and their living motion. Old tones, half-faded, of Dodd and Parsons and Baddeley, have lived again for me at his bidding. Only Edwin he could not restore to me. I have supped with —. But I am growing a coxcomb.

As I was about to say, at the desk of the then treasurer of the old Bath Theatre — not Diamond's — presented herself the little Barbara S——.

The parents of Barbara had been in reputable circumstances. The father had practised, I believe, as an apothecary in the town ; but his practice, from causes which I feel my own infirmity too sensibly that way to arraign, — or perhaps from that pure infelicity which accompanies some people in their walk through life, and which it is impossible to lay at the door of imprudence, — was now reduced to nothing. They were, in fact, in the very teeth of starvation when the manager, who knew and respected them in better days, took the little Barbara into his company.

At the period I commenced with, her slender earnings were the sole support of the family, including two younger sisters. I must throw a veil over some mortifying circumstances. Enough to say that her Saturday's pittance was the only chance of a Sunday's (generally their only) meal of meat.

One thing I will only mention, that in some child's part, where in her theatrical character she was to sup off a roast fowl (O joy to Barbara !), some comic actor, who was for the night caterer for this dainty, in the misguided humour of his part, threw over the dish such a quantity of salt (O grief and pain of heart to Barbara !) that when he crammed a portion of it into her mouth, she was obliged sputteringly to reject it ; and what with shame of her ill-acted part, and pain of real appetite at missing such a dainty, her little heart sobbed almost to breaking, till a flood of tears, which the well-fed spectators were totally unable to comprehend, mercifully relieved her.

This was the little starved, meritorious maid who stood before old Ravenscroft, the treasurer, for her Saturday's payment.

Ravenscroft was a man, I have heard many old theatrical people besides herself say, of all men least calculated for a treasurer. He had no head for accounts, paid away at random, kept scarce any books, and summing up at the week's end, if he found himself a pound or so deficient, blest himself that it was no worse.

Now, Barbara's weekly stipend was a bare half-guinea. By mistake he popped into her hand — a whole one.

Barbara tripped away.

She was entirely unconscious at first of the mistake. God knows, Ravenscroft would never have discovered it.

But when she had got down to the first of those uncouth landing-places, she became sensible of an unusual weight of metal pressing in her little hand.

Now mark the dilemma.

She was by nature a good child. From her parents and those about her she had imbibed no contrary influence. But then they had taught her nothing. Poor men's smoky cabins are not always porticos of moral philosophy. This little maid had no instinct to evil, but then she might be said to have no fixed principle. She had heard honesty commended, but never dreamed of its application to herself. She thought of it as something which concerned grown-up people, men and women. She had never known temptation, or thought of preparing resistance against it.

Her first impulse was to go back to the old treasurer and explain to him his blunder. He was already so confused with age, besides a natural want of punctuality, that she would have had some difficulty in making him understand it. She saw *that* in an instant. And then it was such a bit of money ! And then the image of a larger allowance of butcher's meat on their table the next day came across her, till her little eyes glistened and her mouth moistened. But then Mr. Ravenscroft had always been so good-natured, had stood her friend behind the scenes, and even recommended her promotion to some of her little parts. But again the old man was reputed to be worth a world of money. He was supposed to have fifty pounds a-year clear of the theatre. And then came staring upon her the figures of her little stockingless and shoeless sisters. And when she looked at her own neat white cotton stockings, which her situation at the theatre had made it indispensable for her mother to provide for her, with hard straining and pinching from the family stock, and thought how glad she should be to cover their poor feet with the same, and how then they could accompany her to rehearsals, which they had hitherto been precluded from doing, by reason of their unfashionable attire, — in these thoughts she reached the second landing-place — the second, I mean, from the top, for there was still another left to traverse.

Now virtue support Barbara !

And that never-failing friend *did* step in ; for at that moment a strength not her own, I have heard her say, was revealed to her, — a reason above reasoning,— and without her own agency, as it seemed (for she never felt her feet to move), she found herself transported back to the individual desk she had just quitted, and her hand in the old hand of Ravenscroft, who in silence took back the refunded treasure, and who had been sitting (good man) insensible to the lapse of minutes which to her were anxious ages ; and from that moment a deep peace fell upon her heart, and she knew the quality of honesty.

A year or two's unrepining application to her profession brightened up the feet and the prospects of her little sisters, set the whole family upon their legs again, and released her from the difficulty of discussing moral dogmas upon a landing-place.

I have heard her say that it was a surprise

not much short of mortification to her, to see the coolness with which the old man pocketed the difference which had caused her such mortal throes.

This anecdote of herself I had in the year 1800 from the mouth of the late Mrs. Crawford,[1] then sixty-seven years of age (she died soon after); and to her struggles upon this childish occasion I have sometimes ventured to think her indebted for that power of rending the heart in the representation of conflicting emotions, for which in after years she was considered as little inferior (if at all so in the part of Lady Randolph) even to Mrs. Siddons.

[1] The maiden name of this lady was Street, which she changed, by successive marriages, for those of Dancer, Barry, and Crawford. She was Mrs. Crawford, a third time a widow, when I knew her.

CRITICISMS.

OLYMPIC THEATRE.

THIS theatre, fitted up with new and taste-ful decorations, opened on Monday with a burletta founded upon a pleasant extravagance recorded of Wilmot, the ' mad Lord ' of Roch-ester. The house, in its renovated condition, is just what playhouses should be, and once were, from its size admirably adapted for seeing and hearing, and only perhaps rather too well lit up. Light is a good thing, but to preserve the eyes is still better. Elliston and Mrs. Edwin per-sonated a reigning wit and beauty of the court of Charles the Second to the life. But the charm of the evening to us, we confess, was the acting of Mrs. T. Gould (late Miss Burrell) in the burlesque ' Don Giovanni,' which followed. This admirable piece of foolery takes up our hero just where the legitimate drama leaves him, — on the ' burning marl.' We are presented with a fair map of Tartarus, the triple-headed cur, the Furies, Tormentors, and the Don, prostrate, thunder-smitten. But there is an elasticity in the original make of this *strange man*, as Richardson would have called him. He is not of those who change with the change of climate. He brings with him to his new habitation *ardours* as glowing and constant as which he finds there. No sooner is he recovered from his first surprise, than he falls to his old trade, is caught ' ogling Prosperine,' and coquets with two she-devils at once, till he makes the house *too hot to hold him,* and Pluto (in whom a wise jealousy seems to produce the effects of kindness) turns him neck and heels out of his dominions, — much to the satisfaction of Giovanni, who, stealing a boat from Charon, and a pair of light heels from Mercury, or (as he familiarly terms him) ' Murky,' sets off with flying colours, conveying to the world above, the souls of three damsels, just eloped from Styx, to comfort his tender and new-born spiritualities on the journey. Arrived upon earth (with a new body, we are to suppose, but his old habits), he lights *à propos* upon a tavern in London, at the door of which three merry weavers, widowers, are trolling a catch in triumph over their deceased spouses, —

> They lie in yonder churchyard
> At rest — and so are we.

Their departed partners prove to be the identical lady ghosts' who have accompanied the Don in his flight, whom he now delivers up in perfect health and good plight, not a jot the worse for their journey, to the infinite surprise and consternation, ill-dissembled, of their ill-fated, twice-yoked mates. The gallantries of the Don in his second state of probation, his meeting with Leporello, with Donna Anna, and a countless host of injured virgins besides, doing penance in the humble occupation of apple-women, fish-wives, and sausage-fryers, in the purlieus of Billingsgate and Covent Garden, down to the period of his complete reformation, and being made an honest man of, by marrying into a sober English citizen's family, although infinitely pleasant in the exhibition, would be somewhat tedious in the recital ; but something must be said of his representative.

We have seen Mrs. Jordan in male characters, and more ladies besides than we would wish to recollect, but never any that so completely answered the purpose for the mock Giovanni. This part, as it is played at the Great House in the Haymarket (shade of Mozart, and ye living admirers of Ambrogetti, pardon the barbarity !), had always something repulsive and distasteful to us. We cannot sympathize with Leporello's brutal display of the *list*, and were shocked (not straitlaced moralists either) with the applauses, with the *endurance* we ought rather to say, which fashion and beauty bestowed upon that disgustful insult to feminine unhappiness. The Leporello of the Olympic Theatre is not of the most refined order; but we can bear with an English blackguard better than with the hard Italian. But Giovanni, — free, fine, frank-spirited, single-hearted creature, turning all the mischief into fun as harmless as toys or children's *make-believe*, — what praise can we repay to you adequate to the pleasure which you have given us? We had better be silent, for you have no names, and our mention may be thought fantastical. You have taken out the sting from the evil thing, but by what magic we know not; for there are actresses of greater mark and attributes than you. With you and your Giovanni our spirits will hold communion whenever sorrow or suffering shall be our lot. We have seen you triumph over the infernal powers, and pain and Erebus and the powers of darkness are henceforth ' shapes of a dream.'

Miss Kelly at Bath.

DEAR G——, — I was thinking yesterday of our old play-going days, of your and my partiality to Mrs. Jordan, of our disputes as to the relative merits of Dodd and Parsons, and whether Smith or Jack Palmer were the most of a gentleman. The occasion of my falling into this train of thinking, was my learning from the newspapers that Miss Kelly is paying the Bath Theatre a visit (your own theatre, I am sorry to find, is shut up, either from parsimonious feelings, or through the influence of ——[1] principles). This lady has long ranked among the most considerable of our London performers. If there are one or two of greater name, I must impute it to the circumstance that she has never burst upon the town at once in the maturity of her powers, — which is a great advantage to *débutantes* who have passed their probationary years in provincial theatres. We do not hear them tuning their instruments. But she has been winning her patient way from the humblest degradations to the eminence which she has now

---

[1] The word here omitted by the Bristol editor, we suppose, is ' Methodistical.'

attained, on the selfsame boards which supported her first in the slender pretensions of
chorus-singer. I very much wish you would go
and see her. You will not see Mrs. Jordan,
but something else, — something on the whole
very little, if at all, inferior to that lady in her
best days. I cannot hope that you will think
so, I do not even wish that you should. Our
longest remembrances are the most sacred, and
I shall revere the prejudice that shall prevent
you from thinking quite so favourably of her as
I do. I do not well know how to draw a par-
allel between their distinct manners of acting;
I seem to recognize the same pleasantness and
nature in both. But Mrs. Jordan's was the
carelessness of a child; her childlike spirit
shook off the load of years from her spectators;
she seemed one whom care could not come near,
—a privileged being sent to teach mankind what
he most wants, joyousness. Hence if we had
more unmixed pleasure from her performances,
we had perhaps less sympathy with them than
with those of her successor. This latter lady's
is the joy of a freed spirit escaping from care, as
a bird that had been limed. Her smiles, if I
may use the expression, seemed saved out of
the fire, — relics which a good spirit had
snatched up as most portable. Her discontents

are visitors, and not inmates ; she can lay them
by altogether, and when she does so, I am not
sure that she is not greatest. She is, in truth, no
ordinary tragedian. Her Yarico is the most intense piece of acting which I ever witnessed,
the most heartrending spectacle. To see her
leaning upon that wretched reed, her lover, —
the very exhibition of whose character would be
a moral offence, but for her clinging and noble
credulity, — to see her lean upon that flint, and
by the strong workings of passion imagine it a
god, is one of the most afflicting lessons of the
yearnings of the human heart, and its mistakes,
that was ever read upon a stage. The whole
performance is everywhere African, fervid,
glowing. Nor is this anything more than the
wonderful force of imagination in this performer ; for turn but the scene, and you shall
have her come forward in some kindly, home-
drawn character of an English rustic, a Phœbe
or a Dinah Cropley, where you would swear
that her thoughts had never strayed beyond the
precincts of the dairy or the farm, or her mind
known less tranquil passions than she might
have learned among the flock, her out-of-door
companions. See her again in parts of pure
fun, such as the Housemaid in the ' Merry
Mourners,' where the suspension of the broom

in her hand, which she has been delightfully
twirling, on unexpectedly encountering her
sweetheart in the character of her fellow-
servant, is quite equal to Mrs. Jordan's cordial
inebriation in Nell. I do not know whether I
am not speaking it to her honour, that she does
not succeed in what are called fine-lady parts.
Our friend C—— once observed that no man of
genius ever figured as a gentleman. Neither
did any woman gifted with Mrs. Jordan's òr Miss
Kelly's sensibilities ever take upon herself to
shine as a fine lady, — the very essence of this
character consisting in the entire repression of
all genius and all feeling. To sustain a part of
this kind to the life, a performer must be haunted
by a perpetual self-reference, she must be always thinking of her herself, and how she
looks, and how she deports herself in the eyes
of the spectators ; whereas the delight of actresses of true feeling, and their chief power,
is to elude the personal notice of an audience,
to escape into their parts and hide themselves
under the hood of their assumed character.
Their most self-possession is, in fact, a self-
forgetfulness, — an oblivion alike of self and
spectators. For this reason your most approved
epilogue-speakers have been always ladies who
have possessed least of this self-forgetting

quality ; and I think I have seen the amiable actress in question suffering some embarrassment when she has had an address of the sort to deliver, when she found the modest veil of personation, which had half hid her from the audience, suddenly withdrawn, and herself brought without any such gratifying intervention before the public.

I would apologize for the length of this letter, if I did not remember the lively interest you used to take in theatrical performers.

I am, etc.,

* * * *

February 7, 1819.

RICHARD BROME'S 'JOVIAL CREW.'

The 'Jovial Crew,' or the ' Merry Beggars,' has been revived here [at the English Opera] after an interval, as the bills tell us, of seven years. Can it be so long (it seems but yesterday) since we saw poor Lovegrove in Justice Clack ? His childish treble still pipes in our ears,—' Whip 'em, whip 'em, whip 'em.' Dowton was the representative of the justice the other night, and shook our ribs most incontinently. He was in 'excellent foolery,' and our lungs crowed chanticleer. Yet it appears to us that there

was a still higher strain of fatuity in his predecessor, that his eyes distilled a richer
dotage. Perhaps, after all, it was an error of
the memory. Defunct merit comes out upon us
strangely.

Easy, natural Wrench was the Springlove,—
too comfortable a personage, perhaps, to person-
ify Springlove, in whom the voice of the bird
awakens a restless instinct of roaming that had
slept during the winter. Miss Stevenson certainly leaves us nothing to regret for the absence
of the lady, however agreeable, who formerly
performed the part of Meriel. Miss Stevenson
is a fine, open-countenanced lass, with glorious
girlish manners. But the Princess of Mumpers,
and Lady Paramount of beggarly counterfeit
accents, was *she* that played Rachel. Her
gabbling, lachrymose petitions; her tones, such
as we have heard by the side of old woods
when an irresistible face has come peeping on
one on a sudden, with her full black locks and
a *voice* — how shall we describe it ? — a voice
that was by nature meant to convey nothing but
truth and goodness, but warped by circumstance
into an assurance that she is telling us a lie;
that catching twitch of the theivish, irreprova-
ble finger; those ballad-singers' notes, so vulgar, yet so unvulgar; that assurance so like

impudence, and yet so many countless leagues removed from it ; her jeers, which we had rather stand than be caressed with other ladies' compliments a summer's day long ; her face with a wild out-of-doors grace upon it —

Altogether, a brace of more romantic she-beggars it was never our fortune to meet in this supplicatory world. The youngest might have sat for 'pretty Bessy,' whose father was an earl and whose legend still adorns the front of mine hostess's doors at Bethnal Green ; and the other could be no less than the ' Beggar Maid ' whom ' King Cophetua wooed.' ' What a lass that were,' said a stranger who sat beside us, speaking of Miss Kelly in Rachel, ' to go a-gypsying through the world with ! ' We confess we longed to drop a tester in her lap, she begged so masterly.

By the way, this is the true ' Beggar's Opera ; ' the other should have been called the 'Mirror for Highwaymen.' We wonder the societies for the Suppression of Mendicity (and other good things) do not club for the putting down of this infamous protest in favor of air and clear liberty and honest license and blameless assertion of man's original blest charter of blue skies and vagrancy and nothing to do.

July 4, 1819.

ISAAC BICKERSTAFF'S 'THE HYPOCRITE.'

By one of those perversions which actuate
poor mortals in the place of motives (to
persuade us into the notion that we are free
agents, we presume), we had never till the other
evening seen Dowton [at the English Opera]
in Dr. Cantwell. By a pious fraud of Mr.
Arnold's, who, by a process as simple as some
of those by which Mathews metamorphoses his
person, has converted the play into an opera, —
a conversion, by the way, for which we are
deeply indebted to him, — we have been favoured with this rich novelty at our favourite
theatre. It seems a little unreasonable to come
lagging in with a posthumous testimony to the
merits of a performance of which the town has
long rung, but we cannot help remarking, in
Mr. Dowton's acting, the subtle *gradations* of
the hypocrisy; the length to which it runs in
proportion as the recipient is capable of taking
it in ; the gross, palpable way in which he ad-
ministers the dose in wholesale to old Lady
Lambert, that rich fanatic ; the somewhat more
guarded manner in which he retails it out, only
so much a time as he can bear, to the somewhat
less bitten fool her son ; and the almost absence

of it before the younger members of the family
when nobody else is by ; how the cloven foot
peeps out a little and a little more, till the diabolical nature is stung out at last into full mani-
festation of its horrid self. What a grand in-
solence in the tone which he assumes when he
commands Sir John to quit *his* house ; and then
the tortures and agonies when he is finally
baffled ! It is in these last, perhaps, that he is
greatest, and we should be doing injustice not
to compare this part of the performance with,
and in some respects to give it the preference
above, the acting of Mr. Kean in a situation
nearly analogous, at the conclusion of the ' City
Madam.' Cantwell reveals his pangs with quite
as much force, and without the assistance of
those contortions which transform the detected
Luke into the similitude of a mad tiger or a
foaming demon. Dowton plays it neither like
beast nor demon, but simply as it should be, —
a bold bad man pushed to extremity ; humanity
is never once overstepped. Has it ever been
noticed, the exquisite modulation with which
he drawls out the word ' Charles ' when he
calls his secretary, so humble, so seraphic, so
resigned ? The most diabolical of her sex that
we ever knew, accented her honey-devil words
in just such a hymn-like smoothness. The

spirit of Whitefield seems hovering in the air, to suck the blessed tones so much like his own upon earth; Lady Huntingdon claps her neat white wings, and gives it out again in heaven to the sainted ones in approbation.

Miss Kelly is not quite at home in Charlotte; she is too good for such parts. Her cue is to be natural; she cannot put on the modes of artificial life and play the coquette as it is expected to be played; there is a frankness in her tones which defeats her purposes. We could not help wondering why her lover (Mr. Pearman) looked so rueful; we forgot that she was acting airs and graces, as she seemed to forget it herself, turning them into a playfulness which could breed no doubt for a moment which way her inclinations ran. She is in truth not framed to tease or torment even in jest, but to utter a hearty *Yes* or *No;* to yield or refuse assent with a noble sincerity. We have not the pleasure of being acquainted with her, but we have been told that she carries the same cordial manners into private life. We have heard, too, of some virtues which she is in the practice of; but they are of a description which repay themselves, and with them neither we nor the public have anything to do.

One word about Wrench, who played the

Colonel. Was this man never unhappy? It seems as if care never came near him, as if the black ox could never tread upon his foot ; we want something calamitous to befall him, to bring him down to us. It is a shame he should be suffered to go about with his well-looking, happy face, and tones insulting us thin race of irritable and irritable-making critics.

August 2, 1819.

NEW PIECES AT THE LYCEUM.

A plot has broke out at this theatre. Some quarrel has been breeding between the male and female performers, and the women have determined to set up for themselves. Seven of them, ' Belles without Beaux,' they call themselves, have undertaken to get up a piece without any assistance from the men, and in our opinion have established their point most successfully. There is Miss Carew with her silvery tones, and Miss Stevenson with her delicious mixture of the school-girl and the waiting-maid, and Miss Kelly, sure to be first in any mischief, and Mrs. Chatterly, with some of the best acting we have ever witnessed, and Miss Love, worthy of the *name*, and Mrs. Grove, that rhymes to her, and

Mrs. Richardson, who might in charity have been allowed somewhat a larger portion of the dialogue. The effect was enchanting, — we mean for once. We do not want to encourage these Amazonian vanities. Once or twice we longed to have Wrench bustling among them. A lady who sat near us was observed to gape for want of variety. To us it was delicate quintessence, — an apple-pie made all of quinces. We remember poor Holcroft's last comedy, which positively died from the opposite excess ; it was choked up with men, and perished from a redundancy of male population. It had nine principal men characters in it, and but one woman, and she of no very ambiguous character. Mrs. Harlow, to do the part justice, chose to play it in scarlet.

We did not know Mrs. Chatterly's merits before ; she plays, with downright sterling good acting, a prude who is to be convinced out of her prudery by Miss Kelly's (we did not catch her stage name) assumption of the dress and character of a brother of seventeen, who makes the prettiest unalarming Platonic approaches ; and in the shyest mark of moral battery, no one step of which you can detect, or say *this* is decidedly going too far, vanquishes at last the ice of her scruples, brings her into an infinite scrape, and then with her own infinite good-humour sets all to right, and brings her safe out of it again with an explanation. Mrs. Chatterly's embarrassments were masterly. Miss Stevenson, her maid's, start at surprising a youth in her mistress's closet at midnight was quite as good. Miss Kelly we do not care to say anything about, because we have been accused of flattering her. The truth is, this lady puts so much intelligence and good sense into every part which she plays that there is no expressing an honest sense of her merits without incurring a suspicion of that sort. But what have we to gain by praising Miss Kelly?

Altogether, this little feminine republic, this provoking experiment, went off most smoothly. What a nice world it would be, we sometimes think, *all women!* But then we are afraid we slip in a fallacy unawares into the hypothesis; we somehow edge in the idea of ourselves as spectators, or something among them.

We saw Wilkinson after it in ' Walk for a Wager.' What a picture of forlorn hope, of abject orphan destitution! He seems to have no friends in the world but his legs, and he plies them accordingly. He goes walking on like a perpetual motion. His continual ambulatory presence performs the part of a Greek chorus.

R

He is the walking gentleman of the piece, — a peripatetic that would make a stoic laugh. He made us cry. His Muffincap in ' Amateurs and Actors ' is just such another piece of acting. We have seen charity boys, both of St. Clement's and Farringdon Without, looking just as old, ground down out of all semblance of youth by abject and hopeless neglect, — you cannot guess their age between fifteen and fifty. If Mr. Peake is the author of these pieces, he has no reason to be piqued at their reception.

We must apologize for an oversight in our last week's article. The allusion made to Mr. Keen's acting of Luke in the ' City Madam ' was totally inapplicable to the part and to the play. We were thinking of his performance of the concluding scenes of ' The New Way to Pay Old Debts.' We confounded one of Massinger's strange heroes with the other. It was Sir Giles Overreach we meant ; nor are we sure that our remark was just, even with this explanation. When we consider the intense tone in which Mr. Keen thinks it proper (and he is quite as likely to be in the right as his blundering critic) to pitch the temperament of that monstrous character from the beginning, it follows but logically and naturally that where the wild, uncontrollable man comes to be baffled of his purpose, his passion should assume a frenzied manner which it was altogether absurd to expect should be the same with the manner of the cautious and self-restraining Cantwell, even when he breaks loose from all bonds in the agony of his final exposure. We never felt more strongly the good sense of the saying, 'Comparisons are odious.' They betray us not seldom into bitter errors of judgment, and sometimes, as in the present instance, into absolute matter-of-fact blunders. But we have recanted.

August, 1819.

NOTES.

THE most of the papers gathered together in this volume are taken from the 'Essays' and 'Last Essays of Elia,' and from among the other articles published with Elia's during Lamb's life. The loving industry of Mr. J. E. Babson rescued from old magazines enough of Lamb's neglected writings to make a volume of 'Eliana,' published in Boston a score of years ago. The essays brought to light by Mr. Babson — five of them are reprinted here — have since found place in the later English editions of Lamb's complete Works, whose editors have been able to add a few other forgotten fragments, of which only the dramatic criticisms furnished to the 'Examiner' fell within the scope of this collection. For the grouping of the essays as they appear here the present editor is responsible. For ampler notes than there is need of here, the reader may be referred to the edition of Lamb's Works prepared by his biographer, Canon Ainger, an edition which is a model of wide knowledge, of loving industry, of delicate taste, and of unfailing tact.

MY FIRST PLAY (*page* 35).

To be compared with this essay is a paragraph in the paper on 'Old China,' in which Mary Lamb asks Charles, "Do you remember where it was we used to sit when we

saw the 'Battle of Hexham' and the 'Surrender of Ca·
lais,' and Bannister and Mrs. Bland in the 'Children in
the Wood,' when we squeezed out our shillings apiece
to sit three or four times in a season in the one-shilling
gallery, — where you felt all the time you ought not to
have brought me, and more strongly I felt obligation to
you for having brought me, and the pleasure was the
better for a little shame, — and when the curtain drew up,
what cared we for our place in the house, or what mat-
tered it where we were sitting, when our thoughts were
with Rosalind in Arden, or with Viola at the Court of
Illyria ? "

THE OLD ACTORS (*page* 64).

This paper originally formed part of the essay ' On
Some of the Old Actors,' and is therefore printed here
immediately after it.

ON THE ACTING OF MUNDEN (*page* 68).

Talfourd tells us that Lamb's "relish for Munden's
acting was almost a new sense. He did not compare him
with the old comedians, as having common qualities with
them, but regarded him as altogether of a different and
original style. On the last night of his appearance Lamb
was very desirous to attend, but every place in the boxes
had long been secured, — and Lamb was not strong enough
to stand the tremendous rush, by enduring which, alone, he
could hope to obtain a place in the pit, — when Munden's
gratitude for his exquisite praise anticipated his wish, by
providing for him and Miss Lamb places in a corner of
the orchestra, close to the stage. The play of the 'Poor

Gentleman,' in which Munden played Sir Robert Bramble, had concluded, and the audience were impatiently waiting for the farce, in which the great comedian was to delight them for the last time, when my attention was suddenly called to Lamb by Miss Kelly, who sat with my party far withdrawn into the obscurity of one of the upper boxes, but overlooking the radiant hollow which waved below us, to our friend. In his hand, directly beneath the line of stage-lights, glistened a huge pewter pot which he was draining, while the broad face of old Munden was seen thrust out from the door by which the musicians enter, watching the close of the draught when he might receive and hide the portentous beaker from the gaze of admiring neighbours. Some unknown benefactor had sent four pots of stout to keep up the veteran's heart during his last trial; and not able to drink them all, he bethought him of Lamb, and without considering the wonder which would be excited in the brilliant crowd who surrounded him, conveyed himself the cordial chalice to Lamb's parched lips."

AUTOBIOGRAPHY OF MR. MUNDEN (*page* 81).

This is one of Lamb's most ingenious and ingenuous fictions. It is the Autocrat of the Breakfast Table who tells us that "all generous minds have a horror of what are commonly called 'facts;' they are the brute beasts of the intellectual domain."

BIOGRAPHICAL MEMOIR OF MR. LISTON
(*page* 86).

Lamb wrote to Miss Hutchinson, January 20, 1825, — "But did you read the 'Memoir of Liston,' and did you guess whose it was? Of all the lies I ever put off I value this the most. It is from top to toe, every paragraph, pure invention, and has passed for gospel; has been re-published, and in the penny play-bills of the night, as an authentic account. I shall certainly go to the naughty man some day for my fibbings."

To the Shade of Elliston (*page* 100).

It is to be remembered that Elliston was Mr. H. when Lamb's only acted farce was damned at Drury Lane, and that the actor tried to persuade the author to try the piece a second time.

On the Custom of Hissing at the Theatres (*page* 121).

This essay originally appeared in the third number of Leigh Hunt's magazine, 'The Reflector.'

John Kemble and Godwin's Tragedy of 'Antonio' (*page* 133).

Originally this account of Godwin's theatrical misad-venture was the conclusion of the essay on the 'Artificial Comedy of the Last Century.' It seems to fall into line naturally after the paper on hissing

On the Artificial Comedy of the Last Century (*page* 148).

It was the view Lamb expressed in this essay that Macaulay thought needful emphatically to refute. Matthew Arnold was in the habit now and again of writing about the plays of the day in the ' Pall Mall Gazette,' signing himself ' An Old Playgoer.'   He went to see Mr. Irving's revival of ' Much Ado about Nothing ' at the Lyceum Theatre, and in the ' Pall Mall Gazette ' of May 30, 1883, the ' Old Playgoer ' gave his impression of the performance, incidentally declaring himself to be on the side of Charles Lamb: " So salutary is it to be carried into a world of fantasy, that I doubt whether even the comedy of Congreve and Wycherley, presented to us at the present day by good artists, would do us harm.   I would not take the responsibility of recommending its revival, but I doubt its doing harm, and I feel sure of its doing less harm than pieces such as ' Heartsease ' and ' Impulse.'   And the reason is that Wycherley's comedy places us in what is for us now a world wholly of fantasy, and that in such a world, with a good critic and with good actors, we are not likely to come to much harm.   Such a world's main appeal is to our imagination ; it calls into play our imagination rather than our senses."

BARBARA S—— (*page* 231).

This story Lamb had from Miss Kelly, although he has dressed it up with his usual delight in mystifying his readers.   Two of Lamb's sonnets are to ' Miss Kelly ' and to ' A Celebrated Female Performer in the Blind Boy,' — that is, Miss Kelly.